Betrayal in the Blood

by

Lydia Keys

Betrayal in the Blood

First published in 2012 by
New Dawn Publishers Ltd
292 Rochfords Gardens
Slough, Berkshire SL2 5XW

www.newdawnpublishersltd.co.uk

newdawnpublishersltd@gmail.com

ISBN 9781-908462-10-7

"Do not imagine that the good you intend will balance the evil you perform"

Norman MacDonald

Evil does not lurk in dark corners; it is clear and present for all to see. It is the ignorance which surrounds it that allows it to thrive. Consequently it is only when we experience the injustice of evil directly, do we decide to rise against it.

Prologue

The city is quiet, but he cannot find his peace. Dark rain clouds form above like they did that day, shadows follow his steps like wolves stalking their prey. He was supposed to be getting married today. It was meant to be the happiest day of their lives, but he couldn't help wondering. Who was she, the baby girl on his doorstep, less than a year old? She had come with a note, it was her writing. Had he made a mistake? They had already lost so much, what would be the use in returning for another dose of pain. Every step of the way it felt as though they were swimming against the tide. She was so beautiful and he had wondered if that was what did it. Sometimes he thought it was her beauty that drove her to the edge. She didn't know what it was to be treated normally, people almost fell over themselves to be with her.

Women wanted her opinion, children wanted her love and kindness, men wanted anything she had to offer. Henry just wanted her to himself. She had told him it was out of pity that it happened, that she had felt sorry for him. She knew the effect she had on people, especially men but she couldn't understand why. No-one could explain it exactly. But in the same way that her charm and elegance attracted company, it also isolated her to the point where she was always alone. After all, no-one could ever really understand what it was like.

She had come with a note;

Dearest Henry

Look what we did darling, isn't she wonderful? She is ours to keep from the rest of the world if you will hold me in your arms once more. I made a mistake, it was such a long time ago. I have not stopped loving you dear, though I hate myself for what I did, she is ours. The house is vast and empty without the sound of your voice. Sometimes I think I can see you from up here, wondering amongst the deer. They are restless without you. I write this upon the desk you made for me, do you remember Henry? A wedding gift like no other, you said. You didn't think you could offer the woman who had everything a gift but I was blessed with each day that we shared together.

I have been lost without you Henry but she has your eyes doesn't she? She has my smile. I told her to take it as I barely use mine since we parted, for the last nine months I have lived for her. If you love me darling you will bring her home to me. Bring her home Henry, please. I know you can help me get better. I will wait for three days but if I do not have you both then I must take leave for a while and you will not find me.

I wait for the day I will see you both again my love,

Eleanor

Now he carried the note in his wallet. It went with him everywhere to remind him that it hadn't been some dream, some far away fantasy that he had conjured to escape a painful memory. He wondered today if it was the right thing he was doing. Every day for the past year, he had seen her begin to reflect the beauty of her Mother, the woman he abandoned then too. Every day since the note he had questioned in silence whether he should return. He had not told Nell the truth. On the third day he went there. He saw the red brick wall encircling the grounds for miles, and the deer came to him at the gate. He didn't know what he was going to say or do and then he saw her. Her porcelain face at the highest window, his beautiful queen waiting for him.

She wore her hair long, the beech waves now showing flecks of grey. She was only thirty one. He could almost feel the softness of her lips upon his face, the tender strokes of her long, pale fingers. He remembered how her skin had flushed red during the first pregnancy and how she had retched at each dawn. The aching in his heart every time he reminded himself that she wasn't his. That would never go away no matter how much they loved one another, and by truth he loved her, even now. He could feel her eyes lulling him toward the large oak door but the sadness had rooted itself deep within his body and weighed down his very soul. How could he forget? Even if he went back she would never change. Eleanor would always be beautiful and even as time passed she would grace every room with her presence. He could never look straight ahead no matter how much he wanted to, and she could not refuse to help people, her soul bared too much.

She would not tell him who the father was. She said the baby was a gift to him and something wonderful from a terrible mistake, but she was not theirs to keep. With the baby gone it could have been possible for Henry to forget, to move on to their future. There were moments early in the morning when he could stay lost in her maroon eyes for hours, forgetting anything that came before sunrise, but when they made love it was as though he was sharing her again. Eleanor knew he was troubled. Henry always pleased her in the most loving way but it was afterwards, when he became distant, that she knew they were regressing.

He knew that she had been spending many hours up there where she stood today, writing. Writing what he didn't know. Her guilt had begun to slip out in her moods, some days her emotions would change in the time it took to blink. Henry was out of his depth. He could not help his queen and he could not save them. If he could forgive her she would get better, they would be free to love and live happily, but he could not live half of his life in shadows. It had been the most difficult decision of his life but he knew that if he couldn't have her to himself now then he never really had her to begin with.

Today he would do the same. He hoped that Nell would never tell his daughter the origins of her birth. What child would want to know such misery, such pain. Of course Nell didn't know she was his. Henry had been very careful about who he told his background to. The fact that he couldn't marry her was a realistic reminder that he would never be able to trust any woman again, let alone tell them what he is worth.

This would be his parting gift to Nell, the child that she could never give him, even if he couldn't stay to see her grow.

It was time that he stopped remembering. It was time to stop looking to the past. Today was meant to be his wedding day. Today, Henry Middleton is dead.

Introduction

She recoiled in horror. Not knowing what she was fearful of yet, she slammed the door shut hoping it would retain the information that she didn't want to know. Still, fingers of knowledge were creeping around the door frame, beckoning her closer, closer to the pain, the truth. It had hit her like a brick to the stomach, a blow to top all others. How could she have been so stupid? She sighed in contemplation, staring at the door handle. She did not know what awaited her on the other side but she knew it would change her. Everything in her being told her to turn and run, far, far away and never look back, never even speak of it, but deep within her there was a pull, an invisible cord tugging, willing her to venture through to the unknown.

Yesterday she was Nicole Singer, daughter of Jeffery and Nell Singer. Today she is adopted.

She walks, with every step she retreats further into herself, further away from the past but heading nowhere. She is inside herself, unaware that her path has led her away from the misery at number seven, Prospect Place and toward the city centre. These streets are in her blood, each one running through her veins, mapping her entire body, but she does not know. She knows she is nearing the city as the buildings grow closer to the horizon. There are three buses on the left, one is travelling to Wollaton and she thinks of her father. Her soul shrinks a little more. It was her fault that he left, because she is weak. He didn't give her a chance to fight, the voice of a child lost amongst rowing adults. What is so grown-up about them anyway? They can't agree on minor or major decisions, they don't know how to be happy and when it all gets a bit too much, they run.

She enjoys being coerced by her mind to think about something else and the feeling that her heart had imploded went away, temporarily.

The streets are crowded as she crosses Maid Marion Way and Friar Lane. There is a nightclub on the left. She doesn't understand what a nightclub is yet. She doesn't know that at three am today a couple were mugged as they left the club. She has no idea that people come here to take drugs and copulate. Nicole is ten years old, she has lived a sheltered life which only adds to the shock of what she has recently learned.

The rain beats down hard on the empty market square. It is sparse and vacant like her mind. There are too many questions, too many emotions and she has relented into her subconscious. She sits on the wide grey steps, over shadowed by the Guildhall. There are red banners hanging on either side, displaying future events in Nottingham. They waver in the swaying breeze, making them difficult to read. The fountains to her right are spraying bursts of fizzing water. It is propelled into the air, hissing, and returns with a splash into the semi-still pond below. It is the only sound she can hear.

The rain is lashing at her head but she cannot feel it. She is not sheltered, from anything. She does not benefit from the warmth provided by making herself small, hugging her knees. Today she knows he is never coming back, today she is Bernadette.

***

I roam. I roam because I know she belongs to the city. It is her heritage, her freedom. I live within her walls and I am her citadel from the outside world, and her. She is Nicki and she will survive.

I head towards Jason's house. He will know what to do. He is a good friend and of no threat, he can protect her, love her.

His Mother answers the door, I have been walking for fifteen minutes in the rain and she makes a fuss. I am swiftly taken in, wrapped in a towel and brought in close to her. It is hard to melt into her warm embrace, but she would know something is wrong. I give her five seconds, ease back giving her a smile. "Thanks Rita," I say grinning, and then I ask for Jason. "Yes, he's upstairs, just go on up like you always do," she says with perturbed lines across her brow. I smile again, hoping I haven't drawn too much attention to myself and quickly look to the stairs. They are carpeted in a short thread tan-brown, I learn there is cat somewhere from the long, slightly delicate fur residing there. She has built a wall around Jason, she has not entrusted me with the location of his room yet. I can't ask which room is his, it will draw suspicion. As I reach the top I am faced with a wall. The stairs and the hall make a T shape. I step to the right. "Jase," I say, scouring the different doors. I needn't have bothered. There's a clay door hanger painted with lilac and pink fuchsias, they surround the name 'Jason'. He pokes his head around the door, my sopping feet are sinking into the spongy softness of the carpet. "Hey you, is it raining?" He pulls the door wide open and half runs, half skips to the bay window. Drawing back the dense, black curtains he can see for himself that is in fact raining. The light pours in and he is illuminated. I know everything about this boy and yet I have never met him. All of that is about to change, from now on he will barely leave our side.

"He's gone." I am in a defensive position because that's what I'm doing, I'm defending. Jason is staring at me blankly. "Who's gone?" He eventually says. I know how easily distracted he is so I'm thinking of the quickest way to explain what has happened. We are in Jason's bedroom, which is already donning a certain feminine touch and I wonder if it is Rita's doing or his. He is sitting at the head of his bed upon a cream duvet, the bed is made and he is fluffing a pillow. "My dad," I tell him. I know that he is expecting me to break down, cry and become weak, blame myself, but I can't and I don't. My father left because he was weak, not me. I am still standing, arms crossed, waiting for Jason to say something. "Oh and I'm adopted," I almost laugh. This has his attention but he doesn't know what to say. He quickly shuffles across the bed and stands in front of me, places his hands on my shoulders. "Nic are you ok?" He's looking me dead in the eyes, concern taking over his face. "She will be," I say.

***

She sits alone upon a single bed. It is lonely, bleak. Her room is sparse of furniture and it is plain to the eye. The lino floor is a musty yellow, she has yet to notice the scratch marks meandering from under her bed. She is missing the homely comforts of curtains, cushions and her favorite pajamas. How is it she can remember these things but she can't remember her name?

She writes:

My room is cramped and dark. The small window allows only slivers of light in through the steel bars. I do not know how I got here but I know I am missing, something. I have not seen a single mirror since I arrived here, I do not know what I will see if I happen to gaze upon one. I do not remember my achievements, if I had any but it seems I am quite good at being silent. I have not said anything to anyone, I fear I have done something wrong. Why else would I be treated this way?

I have loved my city, I know every dark corner and illuminated monument in this cruel place.

Snotta Inga Ham was its first name, dating back to the Saxons. It means Man Belonging Village. This was the first thing I learned, and the most important because after that, I knew I belonged to something. My father is responsible for my interest in its buildings, its character and its imprint in history; I have continued to love my city even in his absence. Although he is an architect he taught me to look past the modern distractions or obscenities as he described them, and see the life behind the structure.

I did not find it difficult to imagine the tradesmen travelling from far and wide to sell goods at the market fair. I did not struggle to visualize sinners dangling from a noose outside Shire Hall, even though it has been replaced by a Tapas bar. Every time I visit I can't help but feel outraged. How can someone build an eatery where thousands of people have perished? I make a point of scowling at anyone who goes into the building while I'm there but people just glare at me and carry on. Dad used to ask people on their way into Costa if they knew what it was before being another coffee conglomerate fogging up Britain's culture. Some of them were genuinely interested but most of them just shifted past him as quick as they could manage. Next door to Shire Hall (the gallows) is the Galleries of Justice. Contrary to the name, historical research reports scenes far from any kind of 'justice' here, but as usual the truth is embellished and sold for profit.

My connection to the city is also my connection to him but my love for it comes from somewhere far deeper. It's the way I feel when I'm breathing, the beat of my heart as I pace through its streets, the way I think I can feel its pulse. It's where I belong, with or without father.

It is not unlike any other city in that it has its crime, though it has the highest crime rate in England, with more than equal beauty to its mass, it is a fact to be easily ignored. It is a city divided into sections of love and war, the modern buildings reflecting the surge of plain work houses developed during the Industrial revolution, opposed by the delicate stone work buildings inspired by Roman architecture and later adapted by the Georgian, Edwardian and Elizabethan eras. This city had begun like any other, starting with nothing and building its way through the future. It had built upon a successful industry of wool and silk, the earliest records staring in the Middle Ages.

At the age of ten with a drunk for a mother and a lost, (not wanting to be found) father, this was the first sense of belonging I had ever known. My father never gave reason for his leaving, obviously I blamed myself. After all, what kind of ten year old is confident enough in their ability to be a perfect child wouldn't blame themselves? Now as an adult, I wish I could say that's all in the past, that I forgave myself and my father for what happened. But the truth is I am as damaged now as he must have been when he left. The feeling has never gone away, the feeling of wanting to let go of everything and everyone and start over, knowing that somehow it wouldn't be that much of a loss. I do remember those words leaving his mouth, "it's not your fault Nicole." Whenever I recall that moment it's like something's missing, like he wanted to say more but couldn't, or didn't know how to say it. Perhaps it's just normal for that particular memory to be accompanied by a severe sense of loss as that's what it was; that was the day I lost my father.

I don't remember much from that point. It was like I chose to forget as a way of blocking out anything that might provoke an emotional response. Nell had the same idea. At first she would just drink to help her sleep but soon she was sleepwalking through our lives. We were both grieving but it didn't matter. Somehow she was under the impression that a ten year old can account for themselves, that losing a husband is more hurtful than losing a father, and that I could comprehend, as an adult would, the pain we were both suffering. Or perhaps she couldn't even see through her own pain to recognize mine. I was completely alone and all I had were the streets of Nottingham. That's how I met Jason.

He was everything I wasn't, which is probably why I was so scared of him at first. I thought that if he shared, I shared and although at the time this was not a practice he forced, today he is my closest confidant. Jason was a year older than me which meant that often he acted as my crash dummy. Whenever I was too afraid to try something, (which was often) Jason would offer to check it out first. When I began having panic attacks about leaving primary school to start secondary school, Jason reassured me it would be fun, that we would see each other all of the time and that I wouldn't have to eat lunch on my own or need to make friends because I had him.

He didn't make new friends either, we were two of the same, except that Jason wasn't afraid to show who he was and I hid behind him. Life at home was still unbearable so most of the time I didn't bear it, I stayed at Jason's, Nell didn't even notice. Jason's mum began to see me as an adoptive daughter which didn't go down particularly well with his sister Beth. Fortunately Beth was hitting her teens by then and always seemed more pissed at you than she actually was, and if she was pissed at you it probably wasn't anything to do with you, but you were in the way so you got the sharp end of the stick because somebody had to. Rita was a single mum like mine but she just always seemed to cope better. It meant that Jase and I spent a lot of time in the house alone together but there was always the presence of a mother there. There would be a meal in the slow cooker after school and Jason would wake up to his clothes laid out on the dresser ready for him. I remember thinking how Rita must have felt, coming in from a full night at the care home, sneaking into Jason's room just to make sure he had the right clothes for the next day. How kind, how thoughtful, how Motherly. At night she would tuck us both in and kiss us good night, every night.

Angel of God, my guardian dear, to whom His love commits me here. Be thy always at my side light and guide, to rule and guard.

We Thank you, for we know we are truly blessed Lord.

Until tomorrow

Amen.

Rita knew that I didn't believe in God and she knew I had

my reasons, but she was also a devout catholic. I didn't mind having the prayer said to me every night. Even when I stayed in my own bed at Nell's I found myself listening to the words in my head, surprised that I knew them so well. The truth is they comforted me. I didn't believe that anyone or anything was hearing me but I think there is comfort to be found in asking for help, no matter how subtle. I wish I could live without needing anyone. I long to switch off, give up, sleep. I wish I was strong.

I wish I could call you Mum. I know that if I call you by your name it will somehow make the pain easier to bare. It is a wall that separates us, it removes you from the space around my heart, the space I save for the ones I truly love. Part of me wishes you would find this, but deep down I know you will never care enough to read my diary, or even wonder if I have one. It's wrong Mum. It's wrong that I don't love you. It's wrong that it doesn't break my heart.

Is it possible for the place in which a person lives to transpire into the person? Perhaps I had spent too much time delving into my past; my past is Nottingham's past and I don't know if I can see where one ends and the other begins anymore. It's more than just relating to a place, I feel like I am the place and the place is me. I know every depraved, inconspicuous truth this city has to offer and I have never loved it any less. I could never leave. I had been roaming Nottingham since I was ten years old, alone, searching for comfort within its walls. I remember the first time I entered the Old Market Square.

The Guildhall stands proudly, dominating the entire space. Even now as an adult it towers above me like a proud giant, its protecting lions proudly deferd from each side. The gray flagstone tiles spread out before me, leading to the crumbly old steps of the Guildhall. The fountains to my left interfere with my peripheral sight, the water bursting out into twenty foot jets. It is familiar but every time I come here I get the same feeling; something happened here, a lot happened here but I know this affects me in a way that I can't explain. I feel like I lost something here but I can't remember what it is. How am I so attached by such a sense of loss?

I am distracted from my thoughts by children running around the shallow square pond underneath where the water is falling after being flung into the air. The hustle and bustle of street folk would normally confuse me but I'm steadied by the pure weight and intent of The Guildhall. The square is broad and long, home to goose fairs and strangers trading in the past. People would come from all over England to buy and sell. I close my eyes. I can see brewers and bakers in dirty aprons, blacksmiths, goldsmiths and wheelwrights. They were all here to stake their claim, put their stamp on the world. The carts would begin in the old lace market and line the square. There would be hustlers, barterers, and sellers who were just trying to survive. There's always someone who struggles, always someone who just needs the bare minimum, who can only afford to look to today, not tomorrow. If they think about tomorrow they might give up hope, but they have enough hope to survive today. I know this because I have breathed Nottingham with every breath. It has the stench of survival.

I head towards Trinity Square, cross Victoria street and onto Bridlesmith. It only takes me four minutes to arrive at the Galleries. The tourist board calls it the Halls Of Justice but I know that what happened here and justice are worlds apart. Those poor people, hanged in the name of 'Justice'. A poor sinner, strung up, their family made to watch as they wave goodbye. I couldn't think of anything worse. How does that even work? In 1850 a man could be hung for stealing a loaf of bread, and today we lack a death sentence in Britain for murder. It's totally backwards. I'm not saying I agree with sentencing people to death, but where is the balance? It made my eyes well just thinking about it. It was true, Nottingham had a dark past and a lingering history to match; but however dirty and deprived it was, today it gleamed as if it were brand new, outshining the rest of the East Midlands into a shadowy shame.

I know so much about this city and yet I think I'll never understand it. Maybe that's why I feel so comfortable in its heart and so misguided at the same time. I want my city to accept me, tell me its secrets, perhaps then I would understand my own. I know I belong here but I'm so lost.

Betrayal In The Blood

Chapter One: Getting To Know You

Susie Pierce is a socio-path. Had she not been so skilled at socially conforming, this is the sort of thing she may have seen sprawled across her locker at school. But she was smart. She knew that to be successful you needed people to like you, at first anyway. Once you are at the top it doesn't matter if you're liked or not.

She is not intentionally evil. Yes, she purposefully sets out to get what she wants but she is not aware that the means she uses to do so are considered controversial. The fact that she would use controversial to describe her actions says more about her personality than any profile information on Facebook. She does not consider others when making decisions. She does not have the ability to consider the consequences to her actions. Her impulsive nature means that she is only interested in things and people that can serve her immediate needs and wants. She is a user and once a person has been used up, she discards them without delay or remorse. Of course Susie has very little comprehension that she is sociopathic. She knows that she is different, she can't understand why other people have friends that they can't gain anything from. In this world there are bleeders and suckers. Bleeders give until they have nothing left, and they will still try to give more. Suckers take, they suck the soul right out of the body until there is nothing left. Susie is neither of these. She avoids close friendships as she has nothing to give. She takes, if and when necessary, avoiding human contact when possible. When it's her turn to suck she is inconspicuous, manipulative. To her, knowing how to bleed someone properly is an art form, the trick being that she can always come back for more because they are happy to bleed, even the suckers.

***

Rebecca Pierce raised herself. She was used to being responsible for her success, and from an early age, failure was not an option. At the age of three she learned how to use a microwave, then progressed to cooking a pizza in the oven while her father went away to gamble, coming home drunk to find his little Rebecca had cooked and eaten dinner, brushed her teeth, read herself a bedtime story and put herself to bed. He would ask himself what he had done to bear such an efficient child.

The truth was it wasn't about him. She had been alone as early as the time that she could support the weight of her head and had learned from a young age that she could rely only on herself.

Rebecca did not know she was different from any other little girl her age. She never knew her mother, her father never mentioned her and they did not socialize with other families or children. Preschool was not a priority for Mac, her father so Rebecca educated herself through the means of television. Who needed home tutoring when you had CBeebies Kids? Through her education via the TV, Rebecca learnt numbers, letters, cooking, animals, and interaction, even if it was just with Macaila and the other friendly faced presenters. Rebecca spent many hours of the day alone with the amiable presenters, not knowing how it would affect her in the future. Mac knew that the longer he could keep her out of the public eye the better. He knew that if he let her out of his sight now, it wouldn't be long before people started poking around; "your daughter is very gifted Mr. Pierce." "Your four year old daughter knows how to use an oven Mr. Pierce." "How are you coping being a single parent Mr. Pierce?" This could only lead to one path and he wasn't about to enable it. He was deliberating whether to put her in school or not. If her teachers picked up on how mature Rebecca was they would start digging, something he could do without. Rebecca was his lifeline and he wasn't about to let them get to her. For the first time in his life he had produced something worthy, something marvelous and when it was her time, she would outshine everyone, with Mac by her side.

Mac continued to drink and gamble while marveling at his self-sustaining daughter. Sometimes he couldn't believe how lucky he was, if ever he was down on his luck, a little low on chips he was sure Rebecca would make the perfect settlement. She could cook and clean and kept to herself, she'd make the perfect little house maid, just until he had the money to pay his debts. She did not find it odd that she was at home by herself most of the time. In the moment where she had let her mind wonder and question spending more time with Mac, he told her "Daddy has to go to work to earn money, that's how we eat sweetie." And that was enough. She knew there wasn't any point in crying and complaining when nothing would change.

She had learnt this from the start. The memories were lost to her now, but subconsciously Rebecca knew from being a baby that crying in this house got you nowhere. And she had cried and cried, but only after social services were called did Mac ever do anything. They took pity on him, being a single father and all. "We understand it's difficult for you Mr. Pierce," they sympathized. They did sympathize, but Mac knew that had they been successful in tracking down Rebecca's mother, sympathy would not be on the cards. Mac had to be more careful with his habits. Instead of going out to gamble, he brought the game home where he could desist from abandoning his baby girl. It did not change the fact that she cried, a lot, but it did mean that he could perform the basic care needed to keep him out of jail and keep child benefit in his wallet.

To say he didn't care for his daughter would be misguided. Mac Pierce cared enough for himself and his livelihood and to him that was the crux. No, he didn't want a daughter at first and yes he resented the baby years, but now when he looked at his future he saw all of the things they could achieve, together.

***

At the age of six Rebecca started school. Mac left her at the school gates knowing it was make or break. Would she come across as a happy child, would they find anything sinister? Mac knew there was every chance that Rebecca's efficient nature could arouse suspicion at school, but having Rebecca out of the house for six hours a day meant he could do as he pleased for the most part, before bringing the game home for the evening, and that had to be worth risking one day at school. He would assess the situation after school and, if nothing seemed awry, tomorrow he would enrol her in the before and after school club, gaining him an extra three hours. He stood just outside the school, having parked the car across the street.

"Hi," came a husky voice from his right. He turned around, wondering who it could be. It was a woman's voice. He didn't owe money to any women- actually, right now, he doesn't owe money to anyone. As he turns, he finds himself faced with a beautiful blonde. She wears a paisley print smock dress and a fitted wool jacket, but Mac isn't interested in her clothes. Gentle waves of gold fall about her soft jaw line; he notices her piercing blue eyes as they encroach onto his. He watches her lips, distracted by the pink pout.

"Sorry to startle you, I don't know many people and I saw it's your daughter's first day here. It's Michael's too, my son."

Normally this is when Mac would respond, but he was absorbed by the possibility of sex. To him, what she was saying could only be interpreted as follows; your kid's at school, my kid's at school, we don't have any plans, let's hook up. He decided to see if he was right, knowing full well that he usually was.

"No, it's fine. I don't know many people either. Rebecca, my daughter is far braver than me. She's so strong, don't know where she gets it from." Her eyes smile as they wander over Mac's body. He feigns interest by asking her name.

"Nancy," she replies, holding out her right hand. Her skin is supple, she has long fingers and manicured nails; she is a classic bombshell. He wants her but he isn't prepared to wait around, so he heads back towards the car. "Where are you parked?" he asks. They are standing next to Mac's army green Land Rover now. "I'll walk you to your ca-."

"Oh, no need." She's looking at the floor, maybe Mac had read the signals all wrong, maybe he was losing his touch. "My husband dropped me off." She's biting her lip as though she's already done something she shouldn't have. Within seconds they are embraced, kissing passionately against Mac's tall rover. He fondles the passenger door handle and shoves Nancy inside. She reverses hurriedly into the back seats with Mac straddling her, the heel of her hot pink snake-skin shoe stabbing through the leather interior. Mac drops the seat back and they are out of view.

She tiptoes through the large iron gates. It feels like a fortress. She is apprehended by the feeling that once you walk in you may never walk out. Up to this point, her whole days have been filled with doing her own thing, until Mac arrived home with his drunken gambling buddies. They weren't his friends though, just people, people with money for the taking. She knew her father better than he knew himself. She had been observing him since she was three years old. It was from him that she had learned how to play people. Mac didn't drink when he was alone, but when his 'buddies' were around he drank with them. He didn't know Rebecca, yet around other people he portrayed a fondness for her and kept her close, even involved her, as far as telling her to make sure everyone had a drink in hand, but it was far more than what she got when they were alone together. He would never brush his teeth unless he was going out or someone was coming to the house. When he had dropped her off at school in front of the other parents he'd given her a kiss on the cheek, so much a rare occurrence that she'd almost flinched, would have had it not been for people watching. Now, it seemed the roles were reversed. Rebecca held the power over Mac. She knew far more than Mac estimated. The problem was, Mac still treated her like a baby; sure, it was ok for her to sweep the floor, clean the bath and cook the dinner, but she was too stupid to realize when her father was gunning for sex? She could read Mac like a Sunday paper, he led his life by instinct and he didn't waste a moment on regret.

She found it difficult to tell, but she thought he seemed

anxious on the way to school, asking her how she would introduce herself, what she liked to do, how much she would share. "Share a normal amount; you know like uh, you like to help daddy bake cookies, stuff like that yeah?" He was completely unaware of what he had taught her without intention. In order to see him squirm a little, she had just shrugged and gazed at the floor. "Rebecca, are you listening to me?" His voice now elevated and urgent. She counted a slow, silent count to five, and then looked up into his rugged face. "Yes daddy," she smiled, "I hear what you're saying."

Mac was unusually restless that day. Her first day at school, he supposed it would normally be a joyous occasion, and it was. He supposed most parents would be worried about their kids starting school and having to leave them for the first time, and he too worried, but not for Rebecca. Mac did as he always did, he only worried for himself. But Rebecca was a smart kid, she knew she had it good where she was and he knew she wouldn't do anything to risk that.

It was four thirty, she would be home any minute. Nancy was bringing her home. The doorbell sounded. On opening the door two smiles greeted him on the porch. "Nancy, Hi. Thanks so much for picking up Rebecca, I hope she hasn't been any trouble for you?"

"It's really no trouble Mac, she's been nothing but lovely."

"That's great, Rebecca what do you say to Nancy?" Rebecca turns slowly toward Nancy and says with her sweetest smile, "Thank you for bringing me home *Mrs.* Shepherd, I enjoyed our conversation in the car very much."

There is a shot of concern across Nancy's face, but the thought only lingers temporarily before being chased away by reason. Nancy laughs, "That's quite alright Rebecca, I'll see you again soon."

Rebecca swivels on her heels and heads for the stairs. "Goodnight Mrs. Shepherd."

Nancy is clearly taken aback by Rebecca. "Isn't she just the cutest," she whispers into Mac's ear, "I think she must take after her father." Nancy steps back into the porch, painted red lips smiling. Mac pretends to blush but he's heard it all before; Rebecca was extremely useful when it came to fishing. Mac looks up from the floor coyly. "Will you let me thank you properly for taking care of Rebecca?"

She bites her lip, ponders on her feet for a few seconds then makes her way toward Mac. She grabs him by the shirt and presses her lips onto his, slipping her tongue in for good measure. "You thanked me plenty in the car," she says, pushing up against him, "but you can thank me again any time." She backs away slowly, blowing him a crimson kiss. Mac is smiling, genuinely quite impressed by this woman. As she sways her way down the garden path and into the road, he watches her, marveling over his free pass into Nancy's bed. She turns, giving him one more knowing gaze over her shoulder before she disappears into her car.

Mac is pleased with himself. He still can't believe he is

seeing a woman who drives a 1983 Porsche 911, barely a year old! In truth, it is the only factor determining that he will he see her again. He turns to close the door, smiling broadly, and is met with a presence. She is standing on the stairs, staring at him, still in her school uniform. She is not expressing anything but he knows she has been there the entire time, watching and listening. Mac knows his daughter never misses a trick.

Tuesday 5th March 1985

Testing: Day One
Study: Rebecca Pierce, aged 7

Unofficial Document

It is the end of day one of testing. Rebecca Pierce has returned home with her father, she will not revisit her school until the official report has been processed and the school have made their decision based on any conclusions made in my report. These are rough notes that I am making in my office, after hours due to interference by the patient. Note taking during Rebecca's sessions seemed only to anger her and put stress on the situation and she insisted that I stop. I can recollect most of the interview with great certainty though obviously I will miss minor details.

The most noticeable aspect of the interview is Rebecca's cognitive functioning. She showed very few lapses before answering questions, whether the answer was known or not. She shows the ability to speak fluidly, her use of syntax and length of sentences reach far above the normal average for a girl of her age. I was unable to assess the pragmatics of her speech socially but when one to one she showed a consistent understanding of applied rules in conversation and receptive language.

Behaviourally Rebecca shows accelerated maturity inconsistent with her upbringing, according to national average statistics. She expresses emotional responses consistent with the situational stimuli; for example when shown a DVD of cartoons popular with Rebecca's age group I asked her what she thought about it, her response was "I did not think anything at the time of watching the DVD, I laughed because it was funny and this is a direct, uncontrolled response on my part. In answer to your question Kate, I can only tell you what I think now, after watching the entirety of the DVD, not what I thought during the DVD."

Although everything that she says here makes sense, it is the way in which Rebecca uses words and structures sentences that is cause for concern. Professionally speaking, it is only when Rebecca opens her mouth and speaks that it becomes apparent there could be something wrong. Everything else, her mannerisms, physical appearance (although she is extremely well groomed), and social behaviour coincide with the national average.

Given the knowledge of Rebecca's background, the fact she is in state education, she has been raised by one parent, (whose education stopped at O Level), I must conclude that there is need for further psychological assessment on a weekly basis before I can decide the needs of this child.

"What's all this about?" Mac Pierce was sat in Mrs Hughes

office. Yesterday his daughter came home with an official letter from the primary school. Mac's heart had sunk as his eyes scanned the page. At the bottom, it had been signed by the Head Mistress and Rebecca's teacher. The worst part of the whole thing was that the letter didn't say anything. All it said was that Rebecca had been involved in some sort of incident at school, and that they needed Mac to come in so that they could work towards resolving the issue. He had looked to Rebecca. She stared at him plainly. "What did you do?" he had asked, fearing the worst. Images of Rebecca being carried away by social workers flooded his mind, he'd have to find a job. This can't happen, he had thought.

"I didn't do anything wrong Daddy. One of the other Lady Bay girls stole my watch, all I did was get it back." Mac still couldn't believe that his little Rebecca donned an adult's watch, after clearly showing she was capable of reading time at the age of just three and a half. "So how did you get it back?" He probed, eyebrows raised.

"I thought about what you taught me Daddy. I thought about getting what's mine." Now he was really worried. She continued, "I just told Hilary that stealing does not look good on an application to Oxford and that if she did not return my watch to my hand then I would make sure that all of the prestige universities in England would know that she was a thief. I may have said one or two things about my Daddy knowing certain people who work at the universities too." She never ceased to surprise him, she was becoming more and more like him with each day that passed.

"I don't understand how you're in trouble, they can't tell you off for reclaiming what's yours."

"Am I in trouble Daddy, is that what the letter says?" She had asked him, her face perturbed.

"No that's not what it says but you don't get called into the school for nothing, are you certain there's no more to this story?"

Rebecca shook her head. "You haven't let me finish. When Hilary handed me back the watch I slapped her."

Mac's face dropped. "You slapped her!"

Rebecca was so calm. She explained, "yes, I told her that she comes from a family that can afford to buy her as many watches as there are days in the week and that if she feels the need to steal then it's the first sign of a psychological disorder and that she won't be going to Oxford any way, on account of being crazy. I slapped her because she's stupid and I was angry with her for taking something that is mine." Her arms were folded, and Mac could tell she was fighting the urge to stamp her feet as she spoke. His beautiful daughter. Worryingly intelligent, mature beyond her years and seeming to have little or no sense of right or wrong unless it directly affected her.

"So let me get this right. I have to trek into Lady Bay to talk to your teacher to convince her that my daughter isn't a maniac that goes around hitting people?" He had sounded angry, and he was, but Rebecca didn't fear him. She didn't fear anything. "Ok, this is what we'll do." Mac had proceeded to inform Rebecca of how they would handle this 'slip up', adding that if she must hit people, to only do it when there was no chance anyone else would find out. The next day Mac accompanied Rebecca to school. It reminded him of how much time he had spent in and out of the Head Masters office when he was a kid. He sent her to class, insisting that she apologise to Hilary and make sure she did so in front of witnesses.

Mrs Hughes is staring him down over the top of her tiger-print glasses. "Mr. Pierce, this is a very serious allegation that your daughter faces." It reminds him of being in the Head Masters office when he was at school. He was rarely at school though, that being the main reason for always being called in to see the Head Teacher.

Mrs Hughes could see Mac's mind was wandering. "Mr Pierce, I hope you're taking this seriously," she squinted. He straightened himself. "Yes, of course Mrs Hughes," he says with severe sincerity.

"You can call me Sandra, Mr Pierce, you are not one of the children." She almost smiles. Sandra, no wedding or engagement ring, tiger print frames, school teacher. This is looking more promising by the second, Mac thinks. "Mac," he extends a hand and they linger, holding each other for a little longer than expected. Her hands are soft and warm, her nails are easily maintained with a clear polish. They smile across her desk. Mac's thoughts have turned to other things, things that involve the desk and Mrs Hughes, a school teacher.

This had to be a record. Mac sails through the traffic, oblivious to the horns sounding at him on his way home. He almost couldn't believe it. He's seeing her again tonight even though he has no intention of dating Sandra, only for a repeat performance of this afternoon. He is hoping she will be wearing the glasses, and the pencil skirt, god he loved a pencil skirt. All these women! It's like they feel empowered, they're making the moves on him! Mac silently says a Thank you to Maggie Thatcher.

Rebecca is sitting quietly in the passenger seat. She can't quite work out how Mac has gone from being angry to happy in the space of an afternoon. He wouldn't give details on what happened in Mrs Hughes' office but assured Rebecca that everything was going to be ok, or in his words, "Daddy sorted it." Rebecca had no reason to doubt him, he was the reason they had been ok so far, and though she had never really thought about it before, he had never let her down. She knew that people who did choose to let her down would not be around for very long, she and Mac were running on short threads of trust according to Mac. She didn't exactly understand trust yet. Mac was always talking about people who they could and couldn't trust, and he had made a point of teaching her that Hilary is someone she mustn't trust.

Chapter Two: Better The Devil You Know

I come here every Saturday. It's a long walk from my home in Prospect Place but it's worth it just to get away. I have been coming here since I was ten years old when I had no-one. My mother is a drunk who resents me, but I turn to my city. Opening the secrets to the city will tell me who I am. I have felt lost ever since my father left. He took a part of me with him and I am still the weak little girl he threw away. Nell is deteriorating, she can't cope and I can't cope for both of us.

I moved out at the age of sixteen, Rita offered to house me, I love Rita. It is unfortunate that my own mother won't allow me to love her in this way, she would rather drown herself in drink than look at me. After dad went ,it was like she didn't even want me. She didn't even fight when I told her I was leaving. When someone cares about something, they react. She didn't, it was like I wasn't ever there. I cried in Rita's arms for hours that night, and she prayed and sang to me. Rita told me that some of us are put here to teach others and that others are here to learn. Mine was a lesson in humility.

***

She smiled a long smile. It was the kind of smile to make you bitter. Look at her, I thought, with her waves of beech-coloured locks bouncing around those perfectly defined cheekbones. Those pouting pink lips smirking at the rest of the world. This reality wouldn't bother me so much if I didn't know the truth. This blonde bombshell was exactly that, a ticking bomb waiting to blow up in the next willing victim's face. She was a conniving whore who would do anything to ascend her status and acquire extra equity. If you didn't know Rebecca, you would think she was a saint sent from heaven to make the world less ugly. I did know her, well enough to hate her. As much as Rebecca angers me, it's the idiots she continually manipulates that infuriate me. In the past, I've tried to warn these people, "she's more interested in your wallet than your opinion, your life, your job, you." I even list many of her previous exploits, but they just look at me as though I must be referring to someone else. It's almost like they're under her spell and I'm the only one with an immunity, they just can't see past that bewitching smile.

Rebecca Pierce was engaging her latest conquest. I watched her from across the large ballroom, trying to understand what might be going on in her mind. What might she be thinking? What did she hope to gain? Was she born without morals or were they gradually taken from her as she scurried towards adolescence? Perhaps, whatever the reason was, I could sympathise. The likelihood of feeling any sympathy for Rebecca suddenly slipped away from me as I recalled Rebecca's most recent ploy. Two months ago Rebecca suddenly won a promotion that I had been working for over the past five years. I had been dreaming of a job where I could have my own office, go to meetings and have a real say in the company's future, but no, Rebecca had other plans which as usual involved screwing me over. If she had won it fairly I would still be mad, but at least it would be honorable. Not Rebecca. Jason told me he saw her with Mr. Graham on his way home from Twisters, it was obvious there was more between them than just a drink after work. Again Rebecca seemed to be using her assets to get to the top. If only there was a way to stop her.

Only myself and a few choice friends could see through Rebecca but we all hoped that one day that would change, for good.

I stared into the distance, attempting to appreciate the luxurious décor of the ballroom. A deep purple band spans around the centre of beige walls. Canapés surrounding champagne flutes dress a long table at the end of the room. The golden chandelier offers little light but provides elegance to the occasion and promotes a certain ambience. It was the annual Summer Ball in celebration of the Mayors election. People are filtering in through the large arched oak doors. Most of the women entering are married but have chosen to arrive with much younger escorts, in favour of appearance over integrity. Every year the women would endeavour to outdo each other with their ball gowns. Only the Ladies of higher social standing would know in advance what décor scheme had been planned for inside the ballroom. They prided themselves on standing out as the richest among the middle classes. If they laid eyes on a women whose dress did not complement the colour scheme they would snigger and whisper in the corners, and it would be the subject of all jibing until the following year. I didn't know why I was here. The deep red carpet seemed to fill my head with rage. It charged my thoughts about Rebecca until I succumbed to a stifling migraine.

The Mayor was now attempting to discuss plans for the Christmas village in the Market Square, explaining that the fresh pie stall increased profits by five percent in 2010. I nodded in partial agreement but my attention remained elsewhere. Rebecca was strutting through the crowd as if she was the Lady of the Manor. Her posture was strong, even I had to admit she had been blessed with proportional beauty. If only she could utilise it in a more productive way.

She donned a tight white dress which enhanced her femininity. A golden shawl draped over her structured shoulders, but purposefully failing to hide her visible nipples. The outfit sent a clear message that even at the age of thirty eight, there was nothing old, tired or used about Rebecca. At least, not on the surface. As I examined her from afar I wondered what it would take to make her happy, or at least what it would take for her to stop making everyone else miserable.

Men were approaching her from every angle. Instead of

becoming overwhelmed she took it in her stride, smiling and chatting to each of them one at a time. She could have her pick, no-one second guessed her actions, ever. Lady Penelope scorns her escort on the other side of the room for succumbing to his male nature. They wandered to her like zombies to fresh meat, introducing themselves. Listening to their endeavours to woo her, she was courteous and elegant with her manners, despite knowing that every one of them was ogling her body. To most other women this would be ill-received, but Rebecca understood these gestures as a sure sign she had something to work with. Ever since I can remember, Rebecca had only ever used sex as a weapon. Bribery, rumours, and infidelity all followed shortly after.

Now colour flushes to my cheeks as I realise the Mayor has left. It's likely that he assumes I am disinterested in his affairs, or worse, that I am ignorant to them. I know what I'm doing but I can't help it, Rebecca flips a switch in me that I can't seem to control. I swept the opaque room searching for where my intolerance had sent him. There, I had spotted him. Talking to her. I watched her hands as one gesticulated to accompany her slick words, and the other teased the crystal stemmed wine glass. She caressed it gently, almost as if it was a subconscious movement. I knew that nothing Rebecca was and nothing Rebecca did was ever unplanned.

I stood in disbelief, mentally gawping at this unmerited integration. The Mayor had quite adamantly shared his view with me earlier about 'bunny boilers'. This was the term he had used to describe his ex-wife. He had described her as a hindrance to his politics and a drought to his emotions. Not to mention his wallet. "How does she manage it?" I asked myself. Perhaps everyone could benefit themselves like Rebecca does, only they're not willing to flaunt themselves so blatantly to the highest bidder, I thought.

I couldn't sleep that night. I had lain awake wondering what had become of their evening. Envisaging them lying in a molten embrace. The thought made me feel sick.

Chapter Three: Gossip Inferno

Two days had passed, struggling with my jealousy and anger towards Rebecca. I was beginning to reach the point where I no longer cared when I received a phone call. It was my undisputedly critical friend Jason. "Guess what happened last night?" He poked the question at me excitedly. I knew I wouldn't guess and so did he, but still he waited for me to ask. "What?"

"Pierce's house burned down!"

Quickly I began to judge myself while cruel thoughts of Rebecca's scarred face started filling my head. I pictured her pawing at her lost beauty. I mentally slapped myself. "What?" I beckoned him to elaborate. "After you left the ball, Mayor Troby and Rebecca got into the taxi. No-one knows what their intentions were, though personally I think it was obvious." He paused.

"Yes, I get the point. Continue, please." I asked in a way that was actually telling.

"When they pulled up to Rebecca's house, the whole place was ablaze."

"Then what happened?" My disturbing hopes for a severely injured Rebecca had dwindled, but I could discern that there was more to the story. "Well the fire service had already been called by a neighbour, but the fire was so bad it wiped out everything. Nothing was salvageable." Jason continued to explain how Rebecca had not left the taxi. She just wept into the Mayor's chest as he consoled her in his arms. Sitting silently I contemplated how it must feel to get everything you want and have no-one suspect you.

Soon, everywhere I went there was news of the blaze. Rebecca had conveniently taken refuge in Mayor Troby's house, where neighbours and allies of Rebecca's had congregated to offer their commiserations. I could only think of how wasted their empathy was. They needn't have felt so badly for her.

***

Later the next day, when I would normally be moving on to inwardly console my own problems, I couldn't shift the sickening feeling I had when I thought about how many saps there were in this city. I needed a drink, or several. I had reached the point where all I could do to deal with my severe hand of injustice was to make myself numb. As I stomped along the pavement to my local, I began to feel increasingly comforted by the fact that in less than a few hours I would have little care what I thought, said or did. I needed to let go. Making a beeline for the bar with a self-satisfied smile, I cancelled out everyone and everything else in the room. Peripherals down and blinkers on, I approached the bar. "Whiskey please mate," I said, gesturing with three fingers held up in the bartenders' face. He poured me a large glass of malt and I felt a release as I took the first sip. Savouring the taste, I turned to find a table, a quiet corner I could happily pass out in without being spotted. Perfect. A small round table dimly lit at the back of the pub beckoned me. Strolling over, the other patrons looked like floating, yapping heads. I knew they had bodies but I didn't care, nothing meant anything to me. I looked down at my feet. The carpet was old and worn. It should have been bright and colourful but now after years of being trampled, the faded patterns just swirled together to form a brown and red mass.

I was just getting comfortable when I recognised the smug grin heading in my direction. It was my friend Mickey. I made a silent pact with myself that he wasn't permitted to stay unless he was to join me on the self sabotaging mission I was embarking on. He took up the seat next to me placing his palms down with some force on the wooden table. "I've got something that will cheer you up," he said in his usual all knowing way. "Another drink?" I hoped.

"It's one of those days huh?" He tried to sound sympathetic, but we all knew that the only sympathy Mickey cared about was when it was aimed at him. Only he knows why it's ok to be pitied, why someone would want that. I felt bad enough that I was pitying myself, if someone else joined in it would probably snap me out of it.

"It's been one of those years!" Swigging back the remnants of my drink, I couldn't hide my impatience.

"I shouldn't really be telling you this but I know you won't say anything to anyone about it." His words didn't match the asking expression on his face. I didn't care whether he trusted me or not, I had my own problems. He was still looking at me with raised eyebrows. "Well come on then." I snapped. Taking in a deep breath, he said, "Someone you know took out a hefty insurance policy two weeks before their house blew up." He leaned back in his chair as if he'd just solved Kurt Cobain's murder.

"I can't believe it! Can that woman get anymore sly?" At least I was in the right place to forget about all this crap. Mickey leaned forward, looking me in the eyes. "And she'll get away with it too. My insurance company is paying out a mint and there's no evidence to put her in the frame for arson or anything intentional. Of course no-one's going to question the Mayor's account of what happened, stating that it was an unfortunate accident." Mickey was clearly irritated. He hated his job, but he still hated to see rich people become richer through fraud and deceit. "Except she's not unfortunate in the slightest, is she," I thought out loud.

Mickey was a gem. He was always telling me things about his work. It always stayed in my mind, the way his green eyes flared up when he got (dare I say it) passionate about something. He did get passionate, but about all the wrong things. Most people are excited about days off, learning new topics, going to different places, meeting new people. Not Mickey. He could be put into all of these situations, be the most boring, subtle person in the room and then come home afterwards complaining that he didn't get anything out of it and that everyone hated him (when the truth was they probably didn't even know he was there). But that's what Mickey did, he lacked presence. Sometimes you could literally be standing next to him and you wouldn't notice. God knows I had been caught out by that a few times.

For argument's sake, I guess you could say that his features weren't exactly striking; with his dirty blonde hair, average physique and freckled pallid skin, he didn't stand out from the crowd. He would tell me stories of the latest scandals, of people trying to rip off his company, insurance fraud and people in debt. This was the first story I had been really interested in however. My excitement was dampened when I remembered I was sworn to secrecy. Or was I? Mickey had been trying to find a way out of this job for months. Ever since his boss, Mr. Lucas, had slept with his girlfriend. Imaginably this would be tough to handle for anyone, but for Mickey it was worse. While Mickey made his way to the bar I thought about how I felt for him. Nothing ever really went smoothly for Mickey. He would buy a new car then smash it. He would finally put a deposit down on a new flat then find it had wood rot. He would eventually settle for a girlfriend who wasn't the personification of perfection and she would cheat on him. In my opinion, some people have bad luck, some people have bad days; Mickey had a bad life.

Maybe I would do him a favour. Maybe getting him fired would be a good thing. He couldn't be happy working under the man that stole his girlfriend. Yes, I would be doing him a favour.

Recorded Interview with Bernadette

"It's getting worse Doc, I'm not sure I can sustain this much longer. If I'm not here though, if I don't do this...she won't survive. I can't let her remember Doc, it will kill her."

"Perhaps she is stronger now. Have you thought maybe she doesn't need you anymore?"

"If she didn't need me I wouldn't be here, why do you think I'm here now? Come on Doc, you're supposed to be the smart one, tell me what I'm supposed to do, she thinks she's going crazy."

"I think you should leave. I think your presence is altering her quality of life and that she would cope just fine if you left."

"You didn't see her the day she found out. It broke her James, I was born out of survival and I don't intend on letting her down. It's just, I know she's in pain but I can't let her find out."

"Deep down she knows about you. If you like we could try

some hypnotherapy?"

"So you can get rid of me for good Doc? I won't let that happen. You'll trick her like everyone else has."

"If you let me do the hypnosis it will be in a controlled environment that will allow us to monitor her and keep everyone safe."

"Monitor? You mean poke and prod more like. Don't you think I realise that there's a panel of psych doctors behind that glass?"

"That's ok, they're just learning that's all, we all are."

"Sorry Doc but I think I'm going to figure this one out on my own. If you want to help me you and your little scientist buddies can come up with a way of making this work."

End of Interview

Nicki hated her. Hate was a strong word, a strong feeling for someone like Nicole. She was so nice, so pleasant, such a doormat that people had just got used to the fact that she couldn't say no and that she was so easily manipulated. You almost couldn't blame them, she pretty much invited them to walk over her forehead on a daily basis. Rebecca had used this to her opportune advantage; she had started the job a year later than Nicole and yet today she was being promoted above her. It's not that Nicole didn't wonder how exactly it had happened, it was just that when she answered the question herself, it ate away at her self esteem, or what was left of it. This made her an even easier target for Rebecca, 'what a wimp' she had thought. Besides the fact that she had stolen Nicole's job for under her nose, now she had convinced Nicole, through her own self pity, that it was all her fault, that she wasn't worthy of having a job and that she should just step aside and let the grownups clear her mess.

It hadn't taken much to undertake Nicole, a little badmouthing around the office, a quiet word in the bosses ear. It was all too easy for Rebecca.

***

It is Monday morning and Rebecca is heading to work. The whole department store was modeled on Macy's, but Rebecca would change a few things if she had the opportunity. She knew that one day she would easily be running one of the chains, her boss had already hinted as much. She couldn't wait to leave all the other deadbeats behind, after all they were just getting in the way of her success. It wasn't so bad when she was a personal shopper, when each performance was a reflection of her own abilities, but now her job involved relying on morons to do their jobs properly and she wasn't happy. She took solace in the fact that she could be as rude and detrimental to them as she liked in order to get the job done and her own bosses wouldn't think twice about it. She had noticed though that Nicole Singer seemed to be the worst. She was always daydreaming, away with whatever petty little thoughts the girl had. Nicole did not seem to realise how much this job meant to Rebecca. Perhaps she would have to show her.

The company were trying so hard, too hard to follow Macy's and it didn't work, for some reason, the funding, the staff, who they put in charge up here would never compare to Macy's. When Rebecca had her way it would be better, no-one would need to compare it to anything else because it would be beyond comparison, like her. Her father had pushed her also. He kept asking, "why are you still personal shopping? You should be running the place," he'd say. She knew the only reason he wanted this was for his own personal gain. Mac knew that now, in his old age, he couldn't swindle to the same extent and he needed someone to bring in the cash. As he didn't have anyone else, that person was Rebecca. She had passed Broadmarsh now and was on the doorstep to the building when she saw Nicole. "You're late," she told her. Nicole was always late, she made up for it and surpassed the usual workload when she got here but Rebecca liked everyone to know who was boss. Rebecca smiled, knowing that she too was late but Nicole would never stand up to her.

Nicole's weakness fuelled her power. Within seconds, Nicole was in front of her. "That's a very good observation for someone who's got their head up their arse," she said, and then continued to walk into the building. Rebecca stood quiet for a second and then followed her in, outraged but endeavoring not to show it. Rebecca and Nicole had never got along, although Nicole tried to get along with everyone, they were just so different. Rebecca made her way up the marble steps, it was only eight thirty and she was already getting angry because she couldn't think of a sufficient comeback. The truth was that it had caught her off guard. It wasn't the usual yes sir, no sir Nicole that she so enjoyed torturing five days a week. With each step she desperately tried to strategize what it was she would say, but she just couldn't get over the shock of Nicole's outburst. She decided to be still, for now. As soon as the next adventurous oldie entered the shop and picked up a lacey thong, she would have her revenge.

***

He had left her standing there in the hallway. She was holding the letter from the bank, and the cheque signed E.J.M, and asking about her Mother. Rebecca had never shown an interest before now, Mac had been enough and he had to acknowledge a sense of disappointment when he realised that he wasn't enough anymore. He had managed to quell his anxiety by reminding himself that Rebecca was a teenager now, and at seventeen, she was starting to question him. In all honesty, she had been questioning Mac her whole life; it was only now that she did so aloud. He remembered how she was then, and how she is now.

He had tried his best not to make eye contact with her. He

knows that his daughter knows every trick in the book, he knows because he taught them to her. Had it been his choice, he would have preferred to save a few tricks up his sleeve in case she ever got too clever, but it was too late for that. Rebecca was a fast learner and she had picked up all of Mac's attributes, good and bad.

She is asking him about her Mother. It is only now that she is a teenager that she shows interest. Ever since she was a little girl, Mac has been enough, now she wants to know her origins. Yesterday she had found a cheque for five hundred pounds, it was signed E.J.M and addressed to Mac's account. It had come with a note saying that from next month the payments would be made directly into Rebecca's account, and that the bank needed her details. Next month she would turn eighteen. She would be an adult, in charge of her own money. This had prompted her to question Mac, "Who is this money from? Is it from my Mother, a relative, who? You told me she was dead!"

She had caught him off guard on his way out on another con, this time it was mobile phones. A friend of his had stopped by from Mersey and asked Mac, if they were to come across a lorry load of Motorola's, would he be able to shift them? Mac agreed, it was child's play for him. He was glad to have a break from his poker face, or lack of. At least this way he skipped the risk of being caught cheating, last time that happened he was beaten within an inch of his life. They made sure he couldn't play this side of Lincolnshire. He thought about that day, five years ago. She had only been eleven when he staggered through the door holding his arm and bleeding from his face. She told him afterwards that she barely recognised him, his face was so swollen and bloody. But she wasn't squeamish. Already, even at such an early age, she knew that the sooner they brought the swelling down, the less attention he would draw to himself, and the sooner he would be able to get out and get work again.

It was never about love or feeling empathetic towards her father, Mac knew that. It was about surviving. Rebecca had understood that Mac was her lifeline, without him she would be homeless and hungry and that was as complicated as it got. He looked at her now, she would be eighteen soon and he could lose her. Without needing to rely on him for monetary support, she might just take off. Did he care? Rebecca had been by his side for so long now that it was difficult for Mac to imagine his life without her. The truth was he hadn't been receiving child benefit for her since she turned sixteen, although her Mother had made sure that they didn't go without. Now that money would be going directly to Rebecca, and he didn't even have to ask if she would stick around regardless, he knew the answer already.

Without her, who would cook his meals, who would look after him in his old age, who would clean him up after a bad night? Would his clientele still be so interested in coming over for poker knowing there wouldn't be an attractive young girl to gawp at?

He had to find a way of keeping her here. He would have to pay her Mother a visit.

He was on his way to Rampton, the number thirty two bus was unusually busy this time and he fretted whether he would bump into any disgruntled clients. Luckily for Mac no-one so much as looked at him. He quickly gave himself an ego boost when he told himself it would have been different, hadn't there been some attractive young women on the bus. He had made this journey many times before. Every year the yearning would become too much and he would jump on the bus to see her, but he never saw it through. Rebecca had started questioning lately if her Mother was beautiful. She had very bluntly told Mac that he wasn't attractive and said she must have inherited her beauty from her Mother. He had avoided the indirect questioning and quickly focused on acting upset that his daughter thought he was a brute. This had momentarily defused the questioning but now she was in his head and he couldn't get her out.

She had always told him to be discreet, if he must visit at all. She had been happy to keep correspondence in writing but Mac couldn't stay away, even though this would be the first journey he had completed to see her. At the time of the affair Henry had paid him a serious amount of money to keep it private and Mac always told him as long as it was more than what the vultures could offer then his lips would stay sealed. Mac was an extortionist and he is cold but no amount of money could remove the impact she had left on him. He had seen her reflected in Rebecca with each day that she matured, he knew that soon there would be a queue of men outside his door.

Rebecca had been quick to realise how her attractiveness could serve a purpose. She had seen the women Mac had dated over the years, she had even witnessed them manipulating him a few times. It gave her confidence that one day she would surpass his abilities and have the upper hand. Mac knew she was already grasping the concept of extortion. Why wouldn't she? Rebecca had witnessed it all right on her doorstep for the past twelve years. It was the very reason he was having to take the bus. Rebecca had told him she was using the car for driving practice. Some poor boy had shown an interest in her and now he was taking the morning off from work to teach his daughter how to drive. Of course Rebecca hadn't had to promise or offer the lad anything, it was enough just to be seen with a beautiful teenage girl.

It wasn't worry or angst that Mac felt when he thought of how his daughter would be driving around with a twenty nine year old man. He did not fear for her safety. He had been sure to teach his daughter defensive fighting from an early age, as Mac's father had taught him. No, what he felt was jealousy. There was a time when his daughter had relied on him for everything, and he had given it, in his own way, but now she was branching out. His fear was rooted in the notion that soon he would become obsolete. It was the primary reason that he was going to finish this journey today, he would make sure that Rebecca was not able to go, not yet.

The first time he visited, Mac had been sure to do his research. In order to be discreet, he had performed the research online, his dial up connection had taken forever and he had worried that Rebecca would come home early to see his web search. In all the years they had lived together, Mac had learned very quickly not to underestimate his daughter, after all she had learned from him. The driveway hadn't looked so short in the photograph, and now he panicked, knowing he didn't have as long to gear himself up for what was coming. Had he not wasted time massaging his ego, the three hour bus journey would have been more than sufficient time for this.

"Mac Pierce," he spoke into the intercom. The massive iron gates opened up before him and he stepped through. No turning back now, he thought. For the first time in eleven years, he was in.

Who was this E.J.M? If it was her Mother she had to know- if anything, just to get what she was owed. Mac had always told her that her Mother was dead, which was never a problem, but she had to know. One day she could have a family of her own, and what then? Money was something she wanted a lot of, she didn't need it, she wanted it. He had left her alone, standing there at the age of seventeen, holding the prop to so many questions. Her father had been her teacher,

her mentor, her idol, but now she had been prompted to challenge his information. She could tell when Mac was lying to her- not that he had even tried to lie this time, he'd just left. This was the first time she had challenged him, so consequently he wouldn't suspect that she would be following him.

She had coerced Jimmy into giving her a driving lesson, and meandered very slowly along the three hour journey towards Rampton. It had been easy to stay behind the bus, even with its twenty four stops. She had kept the car at least eight cars behind it, just in case Mac were to dismount or look behind him. It was the way he paused when they arrived at the driveway that caught her. She thought momentarily that he might turn around and clock her, but after a minute he continued forward. He buzzed in at the intercom and strode through the large iron gates, all the while staring up at the barred windows.

Everyone knew of this place. It was famous for being the highest security hospital south of Menston. What the hell was he doing here? Was it even anything to do with the letter she had called him on that morning? Whatever it was, there was no way of her finding out without booking an appointment. Even then, they would only allow relatives in. Was she a relative? She couldn't imagine Mac wasting time on someone he couldn't extort for cash, she knew her father and therefore knew that he didn't have a caring bone in his body. So what was he doing here?

There was no way she would be able to get in without an appointment. She quickly ducked back into the red Fiesta and headed back to Nottingham. On approaching the city they were held by continuous red lights and traffic, cabs and buses in every direction. The zone was double yellow but she didn't have the time to care, and she knew she could talk or otherwise wriggle out of a parking ticket anyway. She pulled in sharply without indicating, Jimmy's face beginning to tighten with stress. He had been so good on the way back, realising that it was not the time to chit chat and that no, Rebecca did not want to make out with him. She would make sure he got a pat on the head and a well done before he dropped her home.

She didn't even wait for people on the pavement to stop or move, she just swung the door of the car out wide, barging five pedestrians clear of the car, causing them to scowl and mutter at Rebecca. Even rushing out of the car, she looked elegant, wearing a grey pencil skirt, denier tights with heels and a ruffle silk white shirt. It hadn't been the best for driving in, but the respect she gained from dressing this way was worth a little discomfort. She had no time to waste on apologies or consideration, and didn't even acknowledge how she had disgruntled them. There was a queue of twenty or so outside the bank but Rebecca was not one for queuing and quickly headed towards the front of the line. A fairly middle aged man waited patiently to be called next, he wore a green quilted waistcoat, wellies and sideburns the length of his face. Rebecca dashed toward him. "I have an appointment Darling, but I'm running a little late." She placed her hand on his lower back, slowly heading south to rest on his upper posterior. She didn't even wait for a reply and quickly continued, "Thank you sweetheart, you're very kind."

"Yes, go on through." the man urged her while vividly searching the room, probably for his wife. Rebecca ran on through to the first available cashier.

Stepping out of the bank into the busy streets, she felt deflated; it wasn't often that Rebecca Pierce did not get what she wanted, one way or another. She thought how ridiculous it was that there was no way of telling who was putting money into your account unless it was a business, and that had been ruled out. The cashier had told her that if this E.J.M was to start putting money directly into Rebecca's account, and if it was done using a direct debit, then they would be able to trace it. Sounded like a lot of ifs to Rebecca and she was impatient for the truth. She knew that if she didn't find out, it would plague her until she did. Why wasn't Mac sharing? Usually it would be to protect himself. Currently he is receiving the money, perhaps he is trying to stop the money from going directly to Rebecca, but why?

***

It was happening, Mac's worst fear was becoming a reality. Rebecca was outshining everyone at school and it was drawing the teachers' attention toward them. She had returned home from school with a letter. It was an invitation to take the eleven plus, but her teacher had added a note.

Dear Mr Pierce,

It has come to our attention that Rebecca is not challenged by the work load provided by Lady Bay Primary. She is often bored in class and rarely gives her classmates the opportunity to perform. Obviously this is not any fault of Rebecca's, however it seems that she may be suited to a different school where the majority of students will have similar capabilities as Rebecca. Perhaps you might consider private education? This is an advisory referral only as Rebecca is more than welcome here at Lady Bay, but I along with her other teachers feel that her needs can be better met elsewhere.

We hope you will consider our advice Mr Pierce, as we believe it is in the best interests of your daughter.

Yours sincerely

Sue David

Great, he thought. His daughter is outshining the bloody teachers. He knew they were right, but Mac had already worked the math in his head, and sending Rebecca to private school would have a serious detrimental effect on his spending. The idea of having a kid was to get paid, not to have to pay out! He would have to talk to Rebecca and teach her a lesson in being humble. What to do with a smart arse daughter? He thought. He would have to show her that sometimes, playing dumb was the easiest way to achieve.

He decided to start off small. She was doing homework in her bedroom, it was immaculately clean as usual. She had already done the dishes while Mac had been reading the letter from the school. "Come on sweetie, we're going out," he told her. "But I need to finish my homework Dad." She didn't even look up as she spoke, she was in preparation for being the ultimate woman, continuing to write while she spoke. "Of all people Rebecca, you do not need to do homework. Come on, I'm taking you to get sweets." He shook his head in awe, how many parents had to use sweets as a bribe to STOP kids from doing their school work? If that didn't scream rare, he didn't know what did.

Reluctantly, she replaced her pencil into the pen caddy and stood up from the wooden desk. "Where will we get sweets from Daddy? You know we can't afford to spend much." She blinked innocently at Mac. He couldn't blame her for being careful, she had been well informed since being coherent that money was tight. Of course it wasn't, but the more Mac told her they didn't have it, the easier it was to have Rebecca on his side as far as his money-earning methods were concerned. Within a few minutes they were in the car. "I thought we'd try somewhere different this time, you can get to know the surrounding towns a little better." She nodded, eyes wide with excitement.

He had left her with specific instructions and dropped her off outside the sweet shop in Beeston. He would drive around the block and pick up at the end of the road in about ten minutes. She was not nervous when she walked in. What Mac had asked her to do was basically stealing, she didn't understand why and she didn't ask; she respected her father and did as she was told. He had left her with the exact money for twenty one penny sweets but she would take twenty five. Each one was lifted and counted slowly into the bag with precision. She carried them with care to the counter and placed in front of the shop assistant. "How many?" he asked her, looking at the bag. "Twenty," she says as she places twenty pence on the counter. He opens the bag and takes a look. She doesn't worry, Mac has told her what to do.

"Looks like there's a few more than twenty in there," he says, looking at the money. "I'm ever so sorry Sir, I was sure I counted twenty," she says, looking into the man's eyes, hers beginning to well now. "My Daddy only gave me this much, please don't be angry with me," she starts to snivel. "It's only a few over kid, no big deal. Here you go." He hands her the bag and smiles. "Thank you so much Sir, you're so kind," she says, her expression changing from sad to surprised and gleeful. She runs out the shop, thanking the man until she is halfway up the street, where she can see Mac waiting in the car. When he saw her half running, half skipping, he thought she may have ballsed it up, then he realised it was Rebecca, not some other parents' half witted child.

She jumped in the car with excitement. "What happened sweetie?" Mac asked. "I didn't have enough money for the amount of sweets you wanted me to get, but the man let me have them anyway, isn't that nice Daddy?" she jibbered. "It's stupid, that's what it is." Mac interrupted. "How so Daddy? The man was just being nice." Perturbed lines now crossed her brow. "And how much is being nice going to cost the shop owner? You were just given five free sweets. How much will the shop owner lose if twenty children come in every week and do the same thing?" She is thinking, he can tell because she is quiet, her brow furrowed. Within a couple of seconds she answered him. "Fifty two pounds a year Daddy," she said, eyebrows now raised. Had he taught her nothing? "Yes that's right, but if I was cross with you what would you say then?" He hoped for the right answer. There was a pause while she thought hard about what it was Mac was trying to teach her, then she answered. "I don't know Daddy." Mac smiled, content that his daughter was no longer a stranger to an easier way of living.

Chapter Four: A Journey In To The Past

Here it is he thought, the day he never thought he would see. Henry Middleton was making his way back, to what he wasn't quite sure. He was leaving his quaint cottage in Derbyshire to come back to the city. He had been barely more than a hermit since it happened. After he left her Henry had situated himself on the grounds at Wollaton, living on the edge of his nerves with being that close. He wanted to know that she was safe, that she wasn't deteriorating. His status as an architect had secured him the job at the renovation and his historical intellect had impressed the contractor. Henry knew how robust and paradoxically delicate Elizabethan architecture was, and he was struck by how Wollaton had been affected by each decade that had passed it by. It was as though Wollaton wore the imprints of time inside and out. He remembered being the only person on the entire site, out of over thirty people, who knew what the gargoyles represented. It was quite unbelievable to him that he alone knew the difference between a gargoyle and a grotesque. If the unspoiled Ancaster stone didn't make it obvious that the decorative figures were gargoyles, he didn't hold much confidence in his colleagues' ability to decipher architecture.

There had barely been any distance between them. Some days he would be working on the slate roof when she was standing at the window. Henry would have to pull his cap down over his eyes, if she saw his eyes she would know. For three months he wrote to his daughter, giving her hope that one day they would be there together, but he feared that day would never come. What if she was as beautiful as her Mother? Would she bring to him the same pain, disguised with such deep love? If she did, it would be no more her fault than it was her Mother's, but it would fall on him to reveal her fate to her. The poor girl, he thought.

The image of her was pinned to the inside of his eyelids, he thinks it will never subside. He hadn't known what to do when it happened, he couldn't give up his guise. They had tried to make it work but how does one get over such a thing? She loved another man, she bore a child to another man. To Henry she had given a piece of herself, a part of her DNA, a part that would never be his, not now. The child had been given to its father on the day it arrived. He should have known then that something was wrong, even a 1950s man such as Henry could tell when his wife wasn't right. It was the way she had just smiled and held her arms out gracefully as they lifted her away, like a gift wrapped toy that would mean more to someone else than it did to her.

He remembered the look on her face in the kitchen. It was peaceful, at ease. She had delivered early and he feared for her life that day, but they did not have a choice. If they had delivered the baby at the Trinity there would have been rumours, and their name would be pitied and tarnished. At this point they had planned to stay together; after all, he loved her more than anything, as if it were some kind of spell he was under. Patiently, he had waited outside of the kitchen until he was called in, and there she was, giving her to the maid. It was only pride that had held him from putting a stop to the whole process, he knew that they had not stood a chance for a contented life had they not seen it through the way they planned. The problem he faced now was that over thirty years later, Henry Middleton still awoke every night trying to convince himself that was the truth.

Now the train rattled along the Derbyshire countryside, the green planes and valleys opening up to please his fancy. He saw himself standing atop a large mound, surrounded by blue sky and the fresh breeze; he took in a deep breath as he lived the moment. His eyes opened suddenly, growing wide with shock, quickly chased by sorrow. It was not unlike that day. The sun had been pouring down on Henry's back as he etched away at the inside of a gondola ring on the south east side. It was his intention to carve his name, somewhere hidden to the outside eye, but where he would know it could stay. This way he knew he would always be a part of Wollaton, and always a part of her.

A sadness had already fallen upon him as he came to realise that she would never be his again, when he heard that scream. One woman's scream among the grumbles of thirty men made it clear to him that she was in pain. Henry descended down the rickety wooden ladder as though his life depended on it, and ran around to the front of the house.

There, below the Prospect room, he saw her feint body dangling from the balcony. Her legs swung back and forth violently as she tried to grasp her footing. The men were all a panic as each one searched the others' faces, looking for an idea of what to do. Eventually a member from the Italian work force wrenched the ladder from Henry's pale hands, and drove it up against the wall to rescue the misguided heiress. Henry's heart was broken in two the day they became separate. Now it was in so many pieces, he dared not try to count them for fear of carrying the pain in his chest. It reminded him like a dagger through his side that he couldn't save his wife or his marriage, even when her life depended on it. That was the last day that either of them spent in the grounds of Wollaton.

***

What a beautiful morning. She was on her way to meet with her solicitor. The fire crew hadn't even made their report yet, but she was confident they wouldn't find the cause of the fire. She was wearing the same outfit that she had worn the night before, with the exception of her coat which felt a little larger than usual. She slipped her gloveless hands into the deep pockets to keep them from the September chill. Her fingers brushed across what felt like a note. She hoped it would be a twenty that she had forgotten about, and became a little excited. When she pulled it out with anticipating eyes searching the paper like material, intrigue replaced excitement.

It was a handwritten note to Nicole. She must have picked up the wrong jacket in her rush to leave the ball, Benjamin hadn't exactly exuded patience that night. She stopped in the middle of the street to read, Sunday morning traffic buzzing by slowly in the background. As she read the first line, she diverted suddenly from her original path and found a bench outside a newsagents. Her eyes never left the page as her body found the seat by pure luck. It wasn't long before she realised that what she held between her fingers now was far more valuable than a twenty pound note. The solicitors would have to wait, the note said to meet him today.

Even if there had been time to consider whether she should do this or not, she wouldn't have. If there was ever an opportunity to have, she would have it, and before anyone noticed. She walked in long strides now, her thoughts getting carried away with the beat of each step. What did he want, why did he leave, why come back now? It was only a fifteen minute walk to the station, but she could do it in ten. She is eager to engage this man, Nicole's father.

Chapter Five: Uncertain Certainty

My father, the man who left us when I was but a baby. I still crave to have him near, to have a Dad that cares and protects. In all the letters he wrote, he made it seem as though he was right here with me. I would write back to him, begging him to see me, to come home, but he said he couldn't leave his work. I knew that being an architect meant working on site but I also knew that, for whatever reason, he didn't want to come home. I blamed myself. I should have let it go when he strayed, but there's a longing within me, the same one that tells me I will always be his little girl. His call had left Nell in a whirlwind. Twenty five long years have passed since he went, twenty five years that Nell has barely survived. Two near-death experiences and many attempts in between, he left her broken.

Now it was happening all over again. Just hearing his voice had given her hope, now she knew that he had not forgotten about us. Nell didn't say what he wanted, only that he wanted to get in touch with me. She had written down an address on a piece of paper, a piece of paper that is now lost. I don't recall leaving Nell's, it's almost as though I woke up in the middle of Derby Road. The shock of hearing her news must have blurred my memory, but I do remember reading a Retford address. If he is in Nottinghamshire, it may be possible to find him. I wonder what it is that he wants. My deepest hope is that he will become a part of my life again, but hope will not help me find him.

He sits alone on platform twelve. If she doesn't come, he will get straight on the eleven-o-five to Derby and forget that he ever came back. Where will he start? 'Sorry' doesn't quite seem enough somehow, he thought. He had to come back, even if it was just to let her know what she is worth. It did not matter if she accepted him or not, as long as she got what she was owed. All this time he had wasted, he hadn't even parented any others. Most of his nights had been filled with nightmares, visions of her haunting face beckoning from beyond the darkness. He took it as a sign that he needed to see Nicole, before it was too late, before they sold it.

She probably hadn't even opened the letters they had sent her. He didn't know if they even gave them their mail, surely if it was a matter of confidentiality they would have to? Was she even in a state to know that she had post? He didn't know, and if Nicole didn't meet him today, it could be lost forever.

***

She made her way from Smithy Row where she had spent the night with the Major, and what a night it had been. She had left him to catch up on his sleep, this afternoon he would be giving his speech on the new shopping mall in Broadmarsh. She passed the Galleries Of Justice, they were holding an open day for the celebration and history of Robin Hood. She often thought of herself as a modern day Robin Hood, taking from the rich and giving to herself. Why shouldn't she have the best of everything too? Canal Street was overflowing with elderlies. Sundays were popular for walks here, even with the brisk weather. Any excuse to leave the house, she supposed. As she approached Carrington Street, the Station came into view. It was a vast grand building, originally built as a military base for the First World War. Its giant clock face chimed, eleven o clock. She stepped in through the massive archway, above her flanks of metal structuring the glass roof. Platform twelve, she knew it well.

Her father used to bring her here as a girl, it was where she had first learnt to pickpocket. Dad always said that, if it was that valuable to them, they'd put it somewhere other than an easily reached outer pocket! He needn't have tried justifying it to her. They had to eat and these train dwellers had the means, to her it was a no brainer. When he had told her that this was the first station to be built in Nottingham, she remembered thinking of all the people that must have been here before her, she wondered how many of them were rich, and how much money she must have missed out on. She told her father that a little home education didn't make up for the fact that she was lacked immortality, to which he'd answered, "We're only ever here for as long as we need to be."

He looked up and down the platform, and then at his Rolex. It was eleven-o-one. His frail heart began to race. He breathed in deeply. In through the nose and out through the mouth, that's what the Doctor had told him. He'd also told him not to participate in any heart-raising activity until after the operation, but this couldn't wait. After all, what if he didn't make it?

The third bench along. There he was. A tall man wrapped in a black suit coat. He still looked as though he was in pretty good shape, medium weight, grey hair slicked back, flecked with white at the front and running through his side-parting. He was looking at his watch, she must be late.

A woman eases herself onto the bench beside him. She is wearing a silky red hair tie, just as he had asked her to in the letter. It clashes with her blonde hair. "Nicole," he greets her. "Father," she lies.

Chapter Six: Seeing Red

It was Friday morning. The week had taken its toll on me and I felt apprehensive about the information I held on Rebecca. How could I use it to pin her? Who could I tell that would use the information to its full potential?

That day at work passed with my mind in a whirlwind of thoughts. Customers came in, I dressed them whilst telling them they looked fabulous. I never thought I was a good liar, but apparently I was adept at bullshitting people. My job was monotonous at the best of times, but today it didn't even feel like I was there. I was on autopilot. My boss insisted, when I interviewed for the job, that being assistant buyer took commitment and flair. Now I know that as long as you can make people feel good, they'll buy whatever you're selling. I was selling whatever it took to get me out of there faster.

5:30 eventually rolled around, and later that evening I met up with Jason. We headed to a swanky new bar down town. It had developed a name for itself as being the latest dive for the upper class mobs to gather. We didn't fit in. My job was to dress the upper classes and Jason was an in-flight attendant, or air hostess as I liked to call him. As much as I mocked him, he loved his job. It had nothing to do with the majors we studied at university, but he was happy nonetheless. Looking back, he had always acted the hostess. Whenever we went out at uni, he would always hand out drinks from a tray and make everyone feel good. The only difference was now he was getting paid for his services.

As we entered the bar, I realised how dark it was inside. I reckoned these yuppies liked not being able to see what was right in front of them. Maybe they would realise what they were if someone turned the lights on and lit up their lives. Jason wasn't worried in the slightest. He wandered on through, swinging his hips through the crowded room. Meanwhile I lingered behind at a sloth's pace, trying not to choke on the condensed clouds of perfume. Smoking had been banned in bars, why couldn't they ban excessive use of pungent liquids too? It's so inconsiderate. It's like these people are forcing me to know something about them when I really don't care.

Before I knew where we had ended up, I spotted Jason standing at the back of a very square room, holding a tray of vodka shots. They were an electric blue colour, my favourite. Jason and I had been drinking buddies since we were fourteen. We had our first beer together by Lake Windermere in 1991. It was the same year Jason told me why we could never be more than just friends, the main reason being that I was a girl. From that day my view of the world changed. I couldn't help but fall for him, those deep brown eyes were enough to melt any fourteen year old. His hair quaffed and shone, a rainbow of browns and blondes in the summer sun. He had perfect pout lips and perfect complexion. I warmed to his gentle silhouette, he was so unthreatening. Perhaps, subconsciously, Jason was enough, just knowing I had a man by my side who didn't want anything from me other than for me to be myself.

I would miss Jason while he was away. For years since we were children he had barely left my side. We were inseparable and although I was blatantly bigger than him, he seemed to think it was his responsibility to protect me. Even at secondary school, when the jocks found out about his sexuality, he turned his attention to making sure it had little or no impact on me. Every day there would be a new remark, "here comes the faggot, backs to wall boys", "mind the step queer boy," often followed by some dick pushing him down the stairs. Their laughter seemed to echo throughout the alleys and corridors, even some of the teachers sniggered. Bastards. They were awful, and to make it worse I'm sure many of them were at least bi-curious themselves. He was so strong though. Any one of those idiots could have beaten him to a pulp (being more brawn than brain) but he sauntered through them, head held high. So many times I wanted to grip his hand, to offer him my support, but he argued it would defy the point of what he was doing, that they would see it as an attempt to cover the truth, to hoodwink them. As if Jason was bothered about what 'they' thought. He didn't even report them when finally one day they beat him up.

Harold Alverston had waited for him by the school gates. He was just out of sight so the kids boarding the bus couldn't see, and neither could the parents picking up outside. He grabbed Jason from behind as he cornered the building, dragging him backwards with his hands over his eyes leaving Jason blinded. Once out of sight and earshot, he continued to punch, kick and bite Jason, telling him that if he ever told anyone about what had happened, next time he wouldn't live to tell the tale. Afterwards at my house Jason recited the story to me while I wept, and he gave me that look of 'I'm not telling the story of the Titanic, save your tears'. He clutched his ribs in pain as he laughed, and told me that it was weird how the whole way through Harold had been sporting a rock hard erection. My mouth gaped as I asked him to repeat, he was mumbling due to his lips being bruised and massively swollen. I had heard correctly the first time. Jason continued to tell me how many 'gay bashers' did what they did because they were afraid of the truth, they were pent up with frustration. Sometimes it was down to religious beliefs, knowing that no one would accept them within their faith. Whichever way you look at it, the fear they have is all for the same reason as Jason, acceptance. Most people want to be accepted, and even if they don't everyone prefers the choice.

Even after we moved out of our flat at university, he decided to buy a house hardly a mile from mine. Oddly, even when he was away at work, he never seemed to be gone for long. I had brushed on the subject briefly on one of the many occasions we had been out drinking. My attempt at subtle questioning had failed severely, so I had to revert to my usual tactless way and ask him questions, point blank. His reasoning for remaining such a huge part of my life was basically, 'if it ain't broke don't fix it'. My response to this rotated around the subject of moving on with his life, settling down, meeting new people and all. However he quite clearly stated that he obtains all of these things from his job as a flight attendant, and that I needn't worry about holding him back. As much as I appreciated this, I still couldn't shake this feeling that Jason thought he somehow needed to protect me. I couldn't imagine why he thought I needed protecting, or what he thought I needed protecting from. I would have to find a more discreet way of probing him if I was to find my answers.

"So French wine? Thought I'd bring a few cases back." Jason's voice pierced my thoughts. We were perched on some pretentious looking stools in the middle of a bar/ dance floor, trying to rest our elbows on what could only be described as a bird table. He was talking about his trip to France.

"Yeah, just don't purchase them until the end of your trip, three weeks is plenty of time for you to sink the whole lot." I told him, fighting to hide my concern that he was leaving me alone.

"Well I'm planning on becoming a more sophisticated drinker while I'm out there. When I get back we can have a wine tasting day!" A small grin crept on to his face as he said the last word. "As if!" we both said simultaneously as we exploded with laughter. What a pompous way to waste alcohol, I contemplated. I'd much rather drink purely for the inebriating effects and regurgitate it later than put it in my mouth and not be able to swallow it!

That night, my alcohol consumption rose. I was quietly

concerned about Jason's sudden decision to leave me alone for longer than usual, and I soon began to encounter the familiar symptoms of intoxication. This was good. I needed to feel numb. I needed to forget the mundanities of my life, even if it was only for a few hours. The hot pink lights above the 'dance floor' began to melt my head. I could feel my body become warm, I could almost feel my blood thickening. I began mentally preparing myself to relax. In an effort to let go of my anger, I somehow managed to become stressed. Thinking about not being angry led me to remembering why I was riled in the first place. That then made me picture Rebecca and all her impurities. I rapidly became enraged as the alcohol fuelled my aggression. I could see Rebecca crying on the mayor's shoulder, sobbing that she was an innocent victim and that she couldn't possibly deserve the cruel hand she'd been dealt. I stormed outside and lit up. Exhaling the white smoke in the crisp night, I hurled my glass at the red brick wall. Jason ran out behind me, he shouted something but I couldn't hear him clearly. I turned on my heels. Jason had a questioning look on his face. "What did you say?" I couldn't quite hear what he had said over the noise of the smashing glass. It sounded like he was calling out to someone else. "I said, wait up Nicki." Jason mouthed at me as if I was stupid.

"Oh." I had been put out of my stride, the sudden burst of anger and alcohol had disorientated me and I felt queasy. With Jason going away and everything else that was going on something about this just didn't sit right, but I couldn't say anything, I had no right to stop him. Exactly, I thought. I'll leave it for now but something's definitely wrong. "What's with the lack of anger management anyway? You were fine a minute ago." Jason had a right to be concerned. "She's just... she's so... she's such a conniving bitch and no-one gets it. She's getting away with fraud as we speak." I spat, working myself in to tears. "Fraud? As in, insurance fraud?" Jason asked, intrigued. "How did you know that?" I hadn't told anyone the secret that Mickey had told me in an attempt to lighten my mood. "Going on past experience I suppose. That woman is capable of anything. If she wants it she gets it." He was right and it made my blood boil. "Yeah, and to make things worse the mayor is now involved too. I was told she lied about everything she had in the house. She even went as far as to tell the insurance company there was a dog locked in there!" I turned from facing the wall to look at Jason. He was texting on his phone. "Are you listening Jason?" I yelled at him.

"Hell yeah I'm listening. This is the best gossip I've heard in years! Soon everyone will know." He smiled, his hand gesticulating a rainbow. "You can't tell anyone. I wasn't even supposed to tell you!" I worried, putting my hand over his phone and lowering it slightly. "It's too late now, six people already know." Jason looked pleased with himself.

After reaching the more-than-unsatisfactory conclusion that Rebecca was never going to get her comeuppance, we decided to return to the bar. I drank to numb the rage, Jason drank in celebration of his fountain of new material to gossip about. I felt helpless and there was nothing I could do.

***

I'm awake, after taking what felt like five minutes to prize my eyes open. For several seconds everything is blurred, but I can smell Jason's cologne. Either we crashed at some else's house and Jason is asleep next to me, or we're at Jason's. I can quite easily eradicate the possibility of waking up in another man's house other than Jason's, I haven't pulled in years and I certainly wouldn't go back to a stranger's house. The first thing I see is the ceiling map, yes I'm at Jason's. After years of Jase and I going out on the town together, he thought it would be useful to know where you are as soon as you wake up in the morning, so he drew a map. There is a large sofa with a large arrow pointing to it with a house drawn around them; 'you are here', the arrow tells me. My temples begin to pound as I lift my head away from the soft plump cushions. *Thud, thud* like a heartbeat in my forehead. I felt rough. I started to feel worse as my eyes stumbled upon what looked like a note from Jason. It read,

Afternoon sweetheart. I had a great time last night, so did you in case you can't remember. It's a shame about the aftermath though. I was most pleased to see you missed the sofa, thanks love. Anyway there's a plane to France awaiting me so I've got to make a dash. Take care sweety, see you in a few weeks.

P.s you don't need to worry, I would never tell anyone.
What was he talking about? I can't remember anything, he

knows me so well. I was wondering what he meant by aftermath, and then something stung my nose. I hold my breath and turn away with a look of disgust as I catch a glimpse of what's in the bucket next to me. My head is pulsating and my eyes are sore. I try to piece together the evening from start to end as I slowly sip a glass of water, but there was nothing. It wasn't the first time this had happened. In fact it had become more and more of a regular occurrence lately. Maybe I would check in with my G.P, see if he could shed some light on the issue. Though he would probably just tell me to drink less and he would probably have a point. The rest of that Saturday afternoon seemed to pass in a blink. I couldn't stop thinking about Jason's note. What was it I had told him? Why could I not remember anything after a night out? Anyone would think I was being repeatedly drugged with rohypnol, at least that's the only thing it seemed similar to.

I'm standing in the bus station thinking about how I'm going to spend my Saturday evening of freedom. Someone has lit a cigarette in the middle of the queue and it's wafting straight up my nostrils. Great. I washed my hair with mango and apricot shampoo this morning, just so that in a few hours' time it can stink of fags. My trail of thought is interrupted by the sound of Nicki's phone ringing. It was Mickey. "Howdy partner!" he almost shouted. I'm put off by his enthusiasm, something I hadn't experienced from Mickey in a long time. "What's up?" I asked, trying to sound normal. "Do you want to get pissed?" he asked excitedly. My first thought was that it probably wasn't a good idea, me being responsible, mixed with alcohol. Then I remembered how down to Earth Mickey was, or to put it truthfully, boring. He wouldn't have any harm come to either of us. The smoke gets into the back of my throat and I begin coughing into the handset. "Are you ok Nic, you're not unwell are you?" I walk to over to smoky Joe and stop directly in front of him. "No I'm not ill, but I am sick of people who think it's ok to smoke in the middle of a bus queue when they know damn well we all have to be in the same place!" I say, taking the nearly finished cigarette from between his fingers and stubbing it out with my tan boots. Mickey's end is silent. He's probably trying to figure out what just happened, a bit like smoky Joe who's just frowning at me, mouth agape. "Yeah why not," I sighed, "meet me at Luigi's in an hour." I spent the next hour listing everyone Nicole knew. I had purposefully chosen to meet Mickey at Luigi's, a bar Nicole had only ever been to once. It had a bad reputation which meant only people she didn't like would be there. Most of the people she knew from work were toffee nosed pricks, and a lot of her friends weren't worth the oxygen they breathed.

Mickey was ok, I suppose. He'd always been there for Nicole and I didn't blame him for being largely a pessimist. Everything he set his eyes on turned to dust in one way or another. I had learned through Nicki's mistakes however that sympathizing with him just fed his weakness. Maybe he would benefit more from a bit of tough love, I thought.

The door opened to the dingy Mexican style bar. A fat cowboy emerged from the doorway and stood in front of me. Why was he looking at me for so long? He pulled up his dirt stained jeans decorated with a large wolf head belt buckle until they sat snugly around his oversized paunch. Did he recognise me? He took a step out into the street and left. Nope, I thought, he's just a pervert. "You can look but you can never touch!" I shouted after him. "Prick." Wound up, I questioned how a man could make a women feel so small with just one degrading look. It comforted me to know that he would probably die of a coronary heart disease someday soon. Disgusted, I opened the door once more. There wasn't anyone in my way this time. As the door opened I could feel every single pair of the forty or so eyes on me. Time stood still as the room fell under a blanket of silence. No-one spoke or listened, they just stared. I studied each face for a reaction to my arrival, other than just the threatening stares because I was a stranger. Nothing. After three seconds the bar returned to normal. Cigars were lit, hats tilted and tongues wagged. Normally I would hate being ignored but I knew this was for the best, and quite frankly twenty or more drunkards rubbed up the wrong way would not have played in my favour.

Quieting my footsteps, I walked through the bar. It was a long room with floor boards and wooden wall paneling. There were tables to my right spreading alongside the wall and up towards the back of the room and a long bar covering the length of the room to my left. Just as I noticed Mickey perched at a table at the very back of the room, another fat cowboy hocked phlegm into his mouth and spat on the floor where my foot was about to land. Coming to a halt, I looked down. Some had gone on to my boot. My favourite black pointed boots. What a jackass. Bending down I rolled up my black jeans on one leg and unzipped my boot. I took it off my foot, walked over to the fat cowboy and smiled at the back of his head while I wiped the phlegm off of my boot on to the arm of his shirt. He slowly turned around with a stern frown across his face. Unperturbed, I smiled at him, "I believe this belongs to you, it's only right that you should have it back." The cowboy slowly stood up from his chair with his fists clenched. As he raised his fist to meet my face, he was grabbed by his wife mid-journey. "Don't you be wasting your energy on this slut," she told him with the tone of being inconvenienced. He took his time sitting back down in his chair, maintaining eye contact with me all the way.

I put my clean boot back on, straightened myself up and headed toward Mickey. On seeing me he sat up straight, waving at me with the pace of an excited puppy's tail. It was obvious he had some good news to tell me, it would be a first. "Hi" I said, sliding in behind the wooden table and sitting down to face him. "Guess what?" he said, ignoring my greeting. "What?" I asked, trying to sound mildly enthusiastic. "You know how my life seems to be in a constant state of perpetual doom?" "Yes," I said, trying to understand why he was wearing a Cheshire cat grin while he was telling me this. "And remember how my girlfriend shagged my boss, Mr. Lucas?" "Yes." I answered slowly not knowing where this was going. If he was trying to make me feel sorry for him it wasn't working, I was just getting agitated. "They're getting married!" He said, gesticulating far too much compared to his usual low maintenance story telling. "Right." I spoke slowly again, hoping that he would get to the point. "They've gone to Paris and they'll be gone for two weeks." he said, the pitch of his voice getting higher every time he spoke. "But you know they're coming back right? And then you'll be miserable again." I told him, hoping he would start talking some sense.

"Wrong!" he yelled pointing his index finger up towards the ceiling. He was beginning to worry me now, I'd never seen him so excited, and neither had Nicki. Then placing both hands flat on the table and looking me straight in the eyes, he said, "When they get back I will be doing Lucas' job! His boss told me something important had leaked and that Lucas couldn't be trusted any more. He wouldn't give me any significant details but I couldn't care less because they're both disappearing from my life and I'm getting his job! Ha! Shove that in your face Lucas, you bastard!" Mickey leaned back in his chair, a man satisfied with his work- finally.

"Well that's great I guess, good for you." I said. Mickey had got his revenge. "Plus now you can afford to buy yourself a girlfriend!" I had to say it. Having Mickey this happy was just too abnormal. It also helped to conceal my anxiety. If Mickey's company discovered the truth about who leaked information about a client, Lucas wouldn't be the only one without a job. Mickey gave me his usual response to my jibes, a sarcastic look as he told me he was going to the bar to find something he could celebrate with. Left alone, I tried to conjure a game plan in case everything went tits up. I had a horrible feeling he wouldn't stay happy for long. Poor Mickey. It wasn't like he didn't try to be successful, he just never managed to get past the halfway mark. I looked over at him, he was chatting up some legs with breasts at the bar. Seeing him this happy, I wondered; could I live with taking away his good fortune?

Chapter Seven: Edge Of Reason

That Tuesday morning, Mickey Marsden walked to work with a smile on his face. It was a first in the five years he had worked in insurance. On arriving, his pretty receptionist handed him a black coffee and advised him that a lawyer was awaiting him in his newly acquired office. Assuming it was related to his recently amended job title, he wandered on in without a care, his mind above the world. Opening the door to his office, his heart sank to the back of his chest. This guy looked mean. He was wearing a tailored black suit, neat and no fuss, which demonstrated he meant business. A navy blue tie tied in a tight knot, black shoes you could see your reflection in, and in front of him on Mickey's desk lay a heavy looking metal briefcase. Everything about this man looked daunting. His eyebrows were thick and black and somehow overpowering. He stood abruptly upon Mickey's entry, towering above anyone under six feet tall, and introduced himself. "Mr. Marsden, I'm Nathan Steel. I'm representing Miss Pierce, I believe she's a client of yours?" he asked with a Scottish accent. Mickey's head dropped. A wave of apprehension hit his entire body. "Yes, of course Mr. Steel. What can I do for you?"

I slept well that night, my conscience renewed. Mickey had called me at work and explained why, for a moment, he had thought everything which had just been given to him was about to be taken away. The mean looking Nathan Steel had asked Mickey to give specific details of Rebecca's insurance policy with his company. According to Mickey, it was clear the authorities suspected her of arson, and were doing everything in their power to cover their backs if indeed that was the case.

Now I could rest assured none of this could lead back to Nicki. If anyone discovered the truth about Rebecca's insurance fraudulence, it was no-one's fault but her own. I had been given a get-out-of-jail free card and it felt great.

***

It was exactly as she had thought but meeting with Jeffery Singer had to proved to me more profitable than she could have ever imagined. They had visited The Rose Garden for brunch and talked for hours. Henry had been surprised that Nicole had not been more stand offish towards him when he explained the truth. Since working with Nicole for the past three years she had an idea of her family life, and she knew it wasn't anything to envy. After all, Rebecca had Mac, who now expected her to look after him in his old age. Mac was still a card shark but he could no longer hold his own if proceedings took a turn for the worse, and after so many years of swindling people, many of whom were his so called 'mates', it demanded him to travel further afield in search of fresh people to con. His age limited him somewhat, and now he looked to Rebecca to rake in the cash and look after him. When Rebecca had laughed in the face of his requests, he had become very angry, spouting off about how he didn't have to raise her, how he could have just left her with her crazy mother and that he had spent his entire life raising her when he could have been doing what he wanted to do. To this, she put the argument forward that Mac had always done what he wanted to do despite having a young daughter to raise, and that it wasn't her fault he'd raised her to be a cheat and a liar and it was coming back to bite him in the arse.

Now she sat in her temporary accommodation at the Major's house with a laptop in front of her. Everything he had told her was true. It had taken five hours of research, chasing one link to another, pulling a few favours from Benjamin, but she had found all of the pieces and they fitted together. She was looking at the Middleton family tree, they were practically royalty! She had to find a way to keep Henry believing that she was Nicole, if she didn't she could lose it all before it was even given to her. It wouldn't be for long, from what he had said she deduced he may only be around for another five months, and even better if the surgery went poorly, it could be five weeks. The best part of the whole plan was that Nicole didn't know a thing about it. Ever since she could remember, Rebecca had been in competition with everyone, pushing herself to the limits to get what she wanted, but finally here it was, and she didn't even need to fight.

I was still going over it two days later on the way to my

G.P's office. I had taken a sick day from work, nobody likes Mondays. Walking into the bright white lounge style office, I was greeted with a knowing smile on Doctor Hammond's face. I wasn't keen on people who smiled at me as though they knew something I didn't. "Nicki, how have you been?"

"Hi Doctor. I've been fine in general but just lately I've noticed I seem to be having trouble remembering things." I didn't want to worry him too much, CAT scans take ages.

"When are you finding your memory is at its weakest?" he asked, leaning forward. "Well to be honest it's usually after a bit of a bender, which to be very honest have been quite regular lately." *Here it comes* I thought, *the telling off*. He looks down at his notes. He is sat with his legs crossed, and now he's stroking his chin as if he's mulling something over. I start to panic.

"Nicole, I'm afraid it is my duty to tell you the same thing that I tell you every time you come to see me."

"What do you mean 'every' time I come to see you? This is the third time I've been here, I don't remember you telling me anything important."

He lets out a deep sigh. I'm holding my breath. I can feel myself getting angry with him but I don't know why. "It just feels like everyone knows what's going on except for me," I blurt out. "Nicole, you have a severe condition which affects your ability to remember certain aspects of your life. The good news is you are in control, you can change everything."

He's smiling at me now, but it's one of those sympathy smiles. I don't need sympathy, I need the truth, why can't I just tell him that? Do I have Alzheimer's, a brain tumour? "Please just tell me exactly what's wrong with me." *Here come the tears, always the tears Nicole. You never could control your emotions.* I could feel my heart pounding in my chest as if it was going to burst through my rib cage. I took a deep breath as Doctor Hammond opened his mouth. He looked uncomfortable. "Nicole, we believe that in an attempt to protect yourself you have invented your own version of the truth, and although it's not exactly hurting you, these methods of protecting you are somewhat... misleading."

Her jaw is slack, some would say she's gone into a state of shock but it happens every time. She'll snap out of it, deny reality, lash out and then it's my turn to fill in. "Is this my fault Doctor, why do you seem angry with me, is that why you're making up these lies, to punish me?" The Doc uncrossed his arms and leaned back, donning a sympathetic look on his face. "Look Nicki, it's not easy living with this sort of condition. We don't even know the full extent of your symptoms. I told you that day two years ago it would be down to you to come and notify us of any changes in your behaviour so that we can learn more and help you deal with it also."

"Deal with it? She can't deal with it. Did you really think I was going to let you tell her James? Didn't you see her response? Vacant, unwilling to accept the truth. I keep telling you she can't handle this!"

"Hello Bernadette." Hammond looked pissed off at my presence but I didn't care. Nicki was way too frail for this. "I have to fix this Doc. I told you how difficult I was finding it last time. I have to make her forget."

"Bernie, I don't advise that at all." He was frowning at me now like my father used to when I'd pretend to singe the cats' tail. "Bye Doc, don't expect be seeing us again." With that I slammed shut the heavy red door for the last time. Nicki didn't need this. She had enough problems gaining focus on her life without this bombshell. If she was allowed to recognize her condition then there was always the chance that she could follow the breadcrumbs back to the beginning. Truthfully, even if she could cope with having the preliminary information, learning the rest would break her. There's nothing worse than having your fears recognized. Jason must be in France. I've been away for one week which means I need to stay for at least another two.

It also means I have to go to Nicki's job while she's absent. Oh joy. A whole fortnight of working with people who she knew didn't like her. The problem was she wanted to be liked by them. Nicki wanted to be liked be everyone, to the point where she was a complete pushover. They all gossiped about her behind her back and she had no idea. "She's in love with her gay best friend," "Nicki can't find a bloke, she'll be single forever," etc. Nicki's problem was that she'd always try to see the good in people when sometimes there just wasn't any. If I had my way every single one of them would get a slap, or worse. Now I have my way and they're not going to know what's hit them. Come Monday, Nicole Singer will no longer have 'mug' written across her brow.

Chapter Eight: Now Or Never

She is crouched behind a Renault Megane waiting for her prey. It might have been easier to poke questions at Rebecca, push her around a little in the car park, but it was too open and Rebecca was apt at playing the victim. It wouldn't work. This had to be done in private, away from potential witnesses, away from Rebecca lovers. She is dressed in black, even the wig is black, her black leather boots have more give in them than she expected, although they are somewhat noisier than she anticipated. It didn't really matter, it would be over before she knew anything had happened.

Calm had left her as she thought on all the areas she wanted to probe Rebecca. Anger came in waves, washing over her like an angry sea. It was the anger that had built over eighteen years of protecting Nicole, but now it was beginning to grate on her. Nicole had been pounded into the sand too many times. She believed she would extract knowledge, some form of understanding which could then be used for Nicole's benefit. She thought about what the Doctor had said, if that's what he could call himself. Was she really putting Nicole in danger? Surely if Nicole had a choice she would choose to have a better life, be respected. She didn't want to think about the truth. That's where she and Nicole were similar, as much as she hated to acknowledge that they had anything in common. Soon the consequences would catch up with her, but she wondered who would be there to take the blame? So far, all she had thought about was the good that she was doing. Things had moved so fast, the planning and plotting, trying to help Jason. Fuelled by anger, the wheels of revenge had started turning, to the point now where they were carrying on by themselves. She had put so much into this she hadn't even stopped to think about if it all went wrong. It was too late now. If she didn't deliver justice then who would? Jason couldn't do it by himself and he had always helped Nicole, more than she knew.

They wouldn't understand, how could they? No-one knows Rebecca like I do. No-one else seemed to see through her like I do. Little by little she's tried to ruin Nicki's life. Perhaps she isn't aware of what she is doing but it's still inconsiderate. I have the chance here to satisfy my intense curiosity and make Nicki's life easier, so why shouldn't I grab that opportunity with both hands? The consequences are great, but the potential extraction of the truth far outweighs them, I can't wait to hear what she has to say.

***

I awoke that morning not knowing what day it was. I felt like sleeping beauty, as though I'd been asleep for weeks. Fragments of what must have been vivid dreams billowed through my head. This was surreal, I had been on an adventure during my comatose state. I couldn't remember anything since seeing my G.P. Still, how much could have changed in a day I thought, trying to reassure myself. If my memory loss had proven a serious problem, I would know. Doctor Hammond was a brilliant G.P and he wouldn't let me suffer. My thought bubble was popped by the sound of the house phone ringing. I wondered if it was Jason calling to inform me about his trip in France. Picking up the phone, I realised it wasn't my lovely comforting Jase on the end of the line. An unfamiliar voice asked, "Miss Singer we need to ask you a few questions. Can we come to your home or would it be easier for you to come to the station?" It was the police. "What's this about?" I asked, confused. "We'd much rather discuss this with you in person ma'am." The gentleman on the end of the line had a firm voice, but he came across as very polite. "Ok, I'll stay put." I agreed.

Replacing the receiver, the consequences of the phone conversation began to sink in. My eyes darted from one side to the other, my cheeks were rosy and I began to sweat. My mind tried to figure what they could possibly want me for while my heart pumped adrenalin around my entire body. The only thing I'd ever done wrong was stealing a few sweets as a kid and bunking off from work every now and again.

Before I realised how long I'd been obsessing for, there were three loud bangs at the door. They seemed so aggressive, bang, bang, bang! Not the sort of approach I would associate with police officers who just wanted to ask questions. I walked to the door, trying to stop my bottom lip from trembling. Two silhouettes were stood outside. I could decipher one was female. I opened the door. "Miss Singer," said the man with the pleasant phone manner. "May we come in?" he said, stepping over the threshold. I didn't see that I had much choice.

My stomach churned as I realised the man wasn't wearing any uniform, which meant one of two things; either they were not the police and I was about to be violated in some way, or he was a detective and these questions they wanted to ask me were more serious than they were suggesting. Immediately I felt intimidated. The women had short blonde hair and bright blue eyes, totally the opposite to my features. I didn't like blondes. 'Never trust a blonde', my father used to say. His eyes were dark and searching. "Could I see some ID please?" I managed to ask, despite my throat going dry. They both presented me with badges. *Detective Myers.* Shit. I would just have to get this over and done with sharply. "Can you tell me what this is about please?"

"Why don't you go and put the kettle on Miss Singer." I didn't really like being given orders but it seemed to make me feel calmer so I headed toward the kitchen. I thought keeping my hands busy would further help me calm down but as o began preparing cups and boiling the kettle my mind started to wonder. *I don't want to be in here making tea*, I thought. *I want to know what's going on, but because a police man told me to do it I'm doing it!* My patience was running thin. I was far too anxious and rushed through it. I marched out of the kitchen, down the hallway and into the living room. I slammed down two cups of tea on the glass table. Just as I began to open my mouth and demand answers the detective placed a picture down in front of me on the table.

It was a photograph of a woman and a boy. The woman had short brown bobbed hair and stood very stern behind the boy, who was almost as tall as she was. She had placed her hands on his shoulders for the purpose of the photo. There were no smiles. The picture had a slightly sinister feel to it. They did not look happy, they seemed almost lost. "Do you know this woman Miss?"

"Please call me Nicki," I asked the detective, somehow hoping to make the situation less formal. Looking closely at the woman's face, my heart sank. I did know her. It was Rebecca. She looked like a different person to the Rebecca I knew now. I had no clue who the boy was. The detective concurred by my reaction that I knew her. "We understand yourself and Miss Pierce did not get along," he accused with a frown.

"You could say that." I said, my defenses rising. "When was the last time you saw Miss Pierce?" His eyes penetrated mine.

"We were at the mayor's ball in South Leigh. She was her usual self." I told him in a very matter-of-fact way.

"That was over a week ago, you haven't seen her since?"

"We're not friends detective, why would I contact her?" I didn't even know why they were here, and it seemed the detective was beginning to question whether or not he was wasting his time. Detective Myers leaned in toward me, his eyes locked on to mine. "Miss Singer." he paused. "Miss Pierce is missing and we need to find her. Items of her clothing and hair were found in a wooded area not far from here. We fear she may be dead. We understand that you work in the same building. You haven't seen her at work?" My face turned white. The blood began to drain from my legs and head. I felt sick. Thinking about Rebecca and all of the nasty things she'd done, I wondered if she was dead because of the kind of person she was when she was alive. I swallowed hard, trying to stop vomit from creeping up my throat. I contemplated who could have done this. The police were obviously treating it as a murder case. The detective and his blonde sidekick stood up.

"I...I, I don't remember seeing her." I swallowed the lump in my throat. The truth was I couldn't remember even being at work. In unison, they placed their badges back in their pockets. "Please call me if you hear or remember anything Miss." said Myers, handing me a card.

"Are there any suspects?" I asked, reaching out for the card with trembling fingers. "We're not able to discuss the case with you at this stage Miss Singer, but again we would appreciate any information you could pass on which may help the investigation." The firmness in his voice helped me to regain my focus. "Of course, good luck." I felt stupid for saying it, but anxiety had got the better of me.

As I closed the door behind them, relief set in. Relief that they were gone. I fell back against the door and leaned against it, feeling that if I stayed there they wouldn't come back. Feeling more composed, my anxiety slipped away from me as my emotions turned to guilt. I thought about Rebecca. Where was she? I pondered whether she may have formed an escape plan whilst the insurance company were on to her. I didn't know, but wherever she was, there lay a possibility she could be out of my life for good. I had to ask myself, did I hate her enough that I'd wish her dead? The fact that I didn't know the answer curdled my blood. I knew I should call Jason and Mickey to tell them what had happened but I couldn't bring myself to speak to anyone. I felt horrid. I slumped down in to the dining chair. I could see my reflection in the polished glass surface of the table. Looking inward I didn't like what I saw. There was a monster brewing inside me and I was beginning to feel out of control. Just then I noticed a cut on my forehead. It wasn't recent but I couldn't think when I'd done it.

Letting out a big sigh, I turned to look outside. The sky was blue, there were wisps of cloud dancing in the space. My tulips bobbed up and down on the gentle breeze. I noticed my washing hanging on the line. It looked dry. Tears began to well in my eyes as I realised I couldn't remember doing that either. I felt I was losing it. Why couldn't I remember the simple things? Had I been so stressed lately that I was forgetting the mundanities of my life? It was possible but far from normal. I stormed outside, picking up the laundry basket on my way through the porch. I attacked my washing, ripping items off the line. My arms flailed at the clothes as pegs flew off in every direction. At this point I would say I was officially depressed. I had no control over my emotions. One day I would be fine, the next I'd have fits of rage. I couldn't even remember what I was doing a week ago and my ability to rationalise my problems was wearing thin.

Throwing the basket on the floor, I dragged my feet through to the living room and picked up the phone. I dialled my work number. Jenny answered with her soft, caring voice and I instantly felt soothed. But I couldn't hold back the tears. "I think I'm having a breakdown," I sobbed. "Nicki? I was worried when you didn't show up for work this morning, what's wrong?" Even when concerned she was still so gentle. "I can't tell you what happened but I think I'm losing it Jen. I need a break. I need your help, can you cover for me please? I can't do it Jenny, I just can't." Poor Jenny could barely make out what I was saying, but she replied. "Ok ok Nicki, it's fine, I'll sort it. Don't worry. Do you need the rest of the week off?" Too upset to even move my lips now, I just emanated a high pitched humming noise. "Thanks." I managed to mumble, before hanging up the phone and covering my face with my hands in shame.

After another hour of sobbing and feeling completely helpless I decided I needed to be around people. Logical thinking had passed, but I thought it may help normality resume if I could be amongst others. Stepping out into the street, my senses heightened. My personal space zone had increased. It stretched three meters beyond me in every direction, I felt fragile. Anyone who entered my zone felt like an intruder. I noticed every little detail, how far away the houses were, the breeze rubbing my ears, the cars in the distance. I felt like everyone had their eyes on me, watching my every move when all I really wanted was to be invisible. Embarrassment washed over me as I realised I was taking tiny footsteps along the gravel path, my feet shaking and intoed. I looked like Bambi. This is pathetic I thought. I need to go home. A wave of shame came over me as I set my sights on my front door, I had only managed to travel 50 yards. With each step home the feeling of worthlessness grew. I needed to talk to someone. Just as I was about to reach the haven that was my front door, I made a decision. It was probably one of the worst decisions I had ever made, looking back.

I took the station wagon keys from the rope around my neck and fell against the truck. My fingers trembled uncontrollably as I tried to fit the key in the rust lock. Eventually it crunched in and turned with a click. The prospect of going somewhere to escape made my heart race, adrenalin coursed its way through my veins until, the wagon began to make the noise. The noise that tells me this inanimate object has lost the will to live. "Come on," I say aloud, as if to spur on the vehicle in some way. "Please." Looking back, it would probably have been better if it had never started, but after five more failed attempts and loud, desperate sobbing, it came to life, barely. Amazingly, I remembered to check the mirrors and signal as I drove off the curb outside my house and towards the city centre.

Chapter Nine: Bad decisions make for Bad people?

I knew there would be nothing left, and if there was then she wouldn't want to share. Nell always was a lone drunk, partly because she had no-one left to drink with, but she would tell you it was her choice to be a loner. Ever since I was a kid she was volatile. Even before Dad left she wasn't a stable person. Dad was the strong one, or at least I thought he was until one day he just upped and left, never to be seen again. Secretly I blame Nell. My mother never could just leave it alone. It's like she wanted to cause a problem out of nothing, picking at a wound until it becomes infected. It was as though she didn't know how to be content.

Dad was always so busy working. He was a specialist builder, working on historical architecture was his passion. When he came in at night she couldn't just say, "how was your day dear?" Instead it was always "where have you been?", "who have you seen?" I'm not sure what she thought Dad had been up to while he was out working to put food on the table and money in her pocket. She's such an idiot. Maybe if she hadn't been so disinterested in Dad, and less accusing, he might still be here, and I might still have a father.

As I signaled off Illkeston Road into Wollaton Street, I was reminded of the first time Dad ever wrote about Wollaton Hall. For months it was all he could talk about, in-between apologizing to me for not being at home with me. The way he explained it, so powerful, so delighted as he recounted the details of the beautiful grounds and its buildings. I was captivated. At ten years old I went there. I roamed the grounds of Wollaton Hall. On the first visit I stayed frozen to the spot in awe at the entrance. It stood majestically four floors high, the four towers on each corner protecting the centre. Grand Elizabethan windows looked out at me, beckoning me inside. I was instantly drawn.

Weeks passed and I spent more and more time at Wollaton. I remember feeling closer to Dad because of it. Even though neither of us knew what the other looked like, spending time at Wollaton, knowing that my father loved the place seemed to form an unbreakable bond between us. It was all I had of him and I still cherish it now. Somehow I felt that I belonged there and it was the beginning of a long indulgent journey into Nottingham's past and my future. My father's interest in Wollaton sparked my interest of historical inheritance and the relevance it has on people and cities today. More than anything I was happy to be taken away from the reality of spending every night from four until nine thirty in the clutches of Nell. "I don't know what your Father's up to but he is never coming home!" she would say to me, as if for some reason it was my fault that he had chosen to put his work before everything else, and that's what had kept him away from us for ten years.

The truth was he simply adored his work. He had found something by looking into the past that sometimes wrenched him away from the present, and Nell couldn't understand. I pondered the idea that wherever he was now, perhaps he was still living in the past. He could be immersed in the life we had together when I was ten, we were a remote family at best but I had a Dad and he loved me. I pulled the wagon into Shakespeare street and parked at Trinity Square car park. I thought about how everything in Nottingham was marked with the past, even street names and car parks. Now on foot, passing the police station on North street, I think of Rebecca.

I cross through Sherwood Street and finally reach my much needed destination. The convenience store offers alcohol at prices that are anything but convenient, but I don't care. I gingerly pick up a bottle of Russian vodka and a small bottle of rum. The thought crosses my mind of adding a fruit mixer to the self-depreciating list, but I'm not in the mood for taking it slow. I leave the shop with lighter pockets and some of the weight shifted from my shoulders. I am relieved that soon I will sleep. Soon I will forget everything, only this time I will be in control. I will choose to forget. I make my way back to the car and then decide to walk. How can I be this organized at getting drunk but I can't even remember hanging my washing out? The confusion begins to stab at my head and all of a sudden the thirty minute walk seems far too long. The quicker I get going, the sooner I can forget my miserable existence.

I have been walking for fifteen minutes by the time I get to Friar Lane. It is busy as usual. The sound of rustling shopping bags and car horns takes over my ear canals. I wonder which coffee chain is precluding the other as I pass Costa and Starbucks. I cannot see any difference between them. Each has students typing away on laptops, other students reading paperbacks and groups of young Italian men talking on their mobiles. Each of the staff are casually going about their duty as 'baristas' behind the influx of customers waiting to be served. How can two coffee shops survive such competitive business when they are right next to each other, and they are practically the same? Apparently people can't live side-by-side in peace, but Costa and Starbucks can.

By the time I reach Castle Boulevard I am back to regressing about my own sorry life again. I know she is the least reliable person in my life but I have relented to self pity, and if anyone is going to help me drown my sorrow, it's my mum. Or as I like to call her, Nell.

I still have my own key so I let myself in. The door to the kitchen still hasn't been replaced after Nell kicked it off its hinges in a drunken rage, and I can see dirty plates and takeaway foils crowding the sink. It is dusk now but inside there are no lights on. To a stranger it would seem as though there is nobody home, but I know she is here. Something stops me as I step past the kitchen. It is as though I have hit a wall. It is dark but I remember this house like my own skin, and there should not be anything in front of me. There is a voice within that tells me not to venture through, gut instinct I guess, but why?

The last time I saw Nell I thought she was dead. I let myself in as I have today, the lights were on, illuminating the piles of dirty laundry and dishes littering the house. The atmosphere was silent, still. I'm standing on what should be an apricot carpet but it's been tainted with years of tobacco smoke, abandoned spillages and dust. I pushed the living room door open. I couldn't see anyone, but the smell of burnt flesh pierced my nostrils, making me want to wretch. Suddenly my eyes were searching the room, like a cheetah stalking its prey I move fast, ducking and weaving around the room. Then I saw her. She had fallen to the floor in a slump at the end of the sofa. Her body was curled up, following the contours of the couch. It was hard to tell through the sheer flower print dress but it looked as though she was bleeding. I rush over and shake her by the shoulders.

"Nell, Nell. Wake up, what happened?" I looked around the room as she moaned. The stench of vodka on her breath was enough to intoxicate a small mammal. I'm surrounded by empty vodka and whiskey bottles. She grabs my hand, "Nicki, is that you? I thought I was dead." At the time, part of me had wished her dead, but on seeing her, so deprived, so needy, I couldn't help but feel sorry for her. It was then that I realized I am all she has. "Nell what happened?" I asked, genuinely confused. It is not unusual for Nell to drink herself into a stupor, even fall and knock herself unconscious, but this was different. Looking more closely at her leg I could see it was seeping with blood and clear liquid, the wound nearly covering her thigh. I needed to inspect it properly but her dress had bonded itself to the sticky fluid oozing from the wound. "I...I must have fallen asleep. I woke up and my leg was burning! I tried to put out the fire but I couldn't stay awake."

"You fell asleep with a lit cigarette again?" I couldn't hide the anger in my voice. Nell was such a liability. Part of me felt that if she wasn't prepared to care enough about herself to be careful, then why should I bother trying to keep her safe. The problem was, Nell didn't care until it was too late, or she was sober. "Don't worry, I'll call the ambulance. You're going to be fine." I stoked her hair which was laced with sweat and grease, it was a long time since Nell had washed. I called the ambulance and with great embarrassment and shame I told them how my mother had fallen asleep with a lit cigarette, set fire to herself and passed out due to shock. They said they'd be ten minutes, I left after five. That was six months ago, and walking in today, I didn't know what I was going to find.

The living room door swings open with a tap. The room is dimly lit by the slivers of daylight creeping through the semi closed curtains. There is a silhouette on the lazy boy. "Your father's been in touch," she croaks. I could be wrong, but she sounds sober.

Chapter Ten: The Unknown

I pick up the receiver in the phone booth at the corner of Citadel and Rifle Street. It smells of urine and empty beer bottles line the floor. Parts of the window lie shattered around the box, I wish I was wearing gloves. I know I'm in deep and the one person I can rely on, the only person that knows the truth, isn't here to help us. My hands are shaking as I put the receiver to my ear and begin dialing. I haven't been this unsteady since the first day we met, the day Nicole found out she was adopted. We met that day and I have never left her. What Nell had told her that day broke her. Everything Nicole had ever known became no more than a story tale. I know how she would have crumbled had she discovered she had been dropped on Nell's doorstep like some kind of unwanted prom baby.

The letters that she had received from Jeffery were real, but he was not her father. The truth was Nell didn't know much about Jeffery. She didn't need to know, his charm and prestige spoke volumes and that was enough. Nell had worked hard all her life. At sixteen she worked at The Playhouse selling cigarettes and snacks. Now she worked as a waitress in one of Nottingham's most prestigious restaurants. It sat on Nottingham's medieval castle grounds, which is why people were attracted to it, but Nell didn't care about that. She cared that even though she was a waitress, at least it was at somewhere fancy. There was a dignity about her the day they met at the fair in the summer of 1981, he was thirty three and handsome. When he asked Nell what she did for a living, she told him with pride that she was Head Waitress at the Rose Garden Restaurant. She went on to explain the importance of the festival to her business, and why she was there. This led her to ask what had brought Jeffery to the festival. He said he had been away from Nottingham for a long time, but that he had always loved the food and drink festival and it brought back happy memories for him. They continued to chat for hours until Nell realized that she was late for work. Nell and Jeffery parted that day not knowing whether they would see each other again, even though there had been a palpable connection. The next day Jeffery arrived at the restaurant with jonquil by the dozen. He said he would like to take her to dinner that evening and she agreed.

Three years later came the birth of their first child, but she was not theirs. A baby girl had been delivered to their doorstep. At first Nell believed it was a gift from Heaven, being that she could not conceive. Jeffery said he knew nothing about where she might have come from and although a reasonable person would have questioned this, Nell was just happy to be a mother. It seemed so perfect then. Now Jeffery was gone and Nicole was no longer hers. Nell could never get away from that fact.

I have to start considering the possibility that soon she may not need me anymore, but for now I'm all she has. The line crackles and croaks. It's ringing, no answer.

"She mustn't know Jason, she must never know. I need you

here, come home. Make it look convincing." I hoped Jason would hear the message before it was too late. She was too vulnerable for me to hold her any longer. Maybe the Doc was right; every time I take the reins she becomes more and more unstable. I can't do this without him.

I walk through the door to my house in Citadel Street and barricade the door with my heavy limbs. My brain feels like it's cracking through the middle, and no amount of relaxation therapy is going to fix it. I know desperately that Nell told me something more than I can remember, but every time I revisit it's just white noise. I have made through to the lounge. On my way to the floor I grab a large bottle of vodka from the cabinet, something tells me I won't be needing a glass. I don't even know if I had a drink at Nell's. I went there to immerse myself in loose hands of alcohol and I have returned more stressed than ever. My head is thumping with every beat of my heart but I don't think it is down to a hangover. A gasp fills my lungs as I take a look at myself. I am sat on the floor in the dark. I never understood before why people do this. They have seats to sit on and lights to switch on but still they choose to ignore them.

Now I know it is because they hide. It's as if the closer you get to the ground, the darker the room, the further away you are from your fear, your loss, the pain. Now I know why she does it, now I am just like her. The high pitched ringing of the phone interrupts my gloom. Probably just another sales pitch.

I limply reach for the receiver and hold it against my face. "Hello, Nicki is that you?"

"Jason." I barely make a whisper. "I'm just...the police have been here. I think I'm losing my mind." I whimpered. " I'm coming home," he told me, and hung up. Hope. It was something barely recognizable to me, something I felt I hadn't had in very long time.

Jason arrived the next day. He had let himself in with my spare set of keys to find me sat on the floor in front of the sofa, curled up in a ball. He knelt down in front of me and tried to look me in the eyes. "Nic you look terrible. Have you even slept since yesterday?" I shook my head no. I couldn't bring myself to speak. I felt pathetic. "Nicki I can't help you unless you tell me what happened. What did the police say?" It sounded as though Jason was worried. He seemed anxious that I may be in trouble and wanted to know exactly what the police had asked me. "Rebecca is missing, they're treating it as a murder case. They found her clothes in the woods," I said, sniffling. "Oh shit." Jason suddenly looked stressed. "What have you got to do with any of it?" he asked, confused. "They just want information. I couldn't give them any." I replied, still feeling totally helpless. Then there was a loud knock at the door. I looked at Jason, he could tell I was afraid. Jason wondered over to the door and opened it.

I exhaled as I saw Mickey stood in the doorway. He walked in, and on seeing me sat on the floor in a heaped mess he said in his usual tactful manner, "What's the matter with you? Why are you sat on the floor looking like shit?" I got up slowly and slumbered in to the kitchen. "I'm making tea if anyone wants one," I mumbled without waiting for a reply. You can always rely on good old tea when the shit hits the fan, I thought. I could hear Jason filling in Mickey on everything that had happened while I distracted myself scalding tea bags with boiling water. "I'm surprised I hadn't heard any of this from you yesterday mate. Usually you're texting everyone the minute you hear something juicy," Mickey said to Jason as I re-entered the living room. "This is different," Jason said, shrugging his shoulders. "It's a sensitive issue." "Doesn't normally stop you." Mickey muttered under his breath. "Anyway Nic, I reckon you could do with a drink after all that nonsense with the police. Jason, did you bring any wine back with you?"

Mickey was trying to lift the atmosphere. I couldn't blame him, it felt terrible. The air was thick with stagnant sadness, anxiety and confusion, last night it had been raw with emotion. "Did I? Of course I did, I've got a whole crate sitting at home. I made sure I got the stuff they drink, not the crap they usually give to us. I'll be back in ten," Jason said enthusiastically as he hopped through the door. While Jason was gone I went around my living room with a box of matches, lighting all of my candles. The evening was setting in and I felt candles would help alleviate the mood. I turned to place a candle on the circular coffee table and found Mickey stood in front of me. "Alright," I said, wondering what he was doing. "Yeah, but you're not," he said as he threw his arms around me and pulled me in tight.

At this point I was actually feeling a lot better, but I knew how important it was to Mickey that he felt he was being supportive. Receiving a bear hug from Mickey was his way of showing me he cared. He could never seem to just say the words or voice his emotions. So, physically squeezing the breath from my lungs was the best I could hope for from Mickey. For a few seconds I felt safe, like he was absorbing all of my pain. For that brief interval it didn't seem to matter that there were things I didn't understand about myself. I didn't feel lonely and as he held me tight I let myself relax into his arms. His breathing was slow and deep. Mimicking the pattern, I began to feel calm. It felt good. A couple of minutes passed while it felt like time had stood still. We pulled away from each other and I smiled a satisfied smile as Mickey placed his hands on my shoulders and lowered his head to look me in the eyes. He didn't say anything, but on realising I was happier he smiled too.

"You'll be ok," he said knowingly, rubbing his arms. I nodded. "I know." We both turned to look at the door as we heard Jason approaching. "So, I didn't know what everyone was in the mood for, so I brought three of each," he gasped, walking into the living room and placing a carrier on the floor. "Shiraz I hope? I can't handle another bad hang over." I stated. "Of course of course," Jason repeated as if he was insulted by my inquiry. We sat down at the table with a deck of cards and what would probably amount to a bottle of wine each. The scented candles added warmth to the room and filled the air with sweet vanilla. I leaned back into my chair. In the company of my two best friends in my warm living room, I felt better than I had in weeks. You might say I felt untouchable.

I'd had two glasses of wine and was feeling mildly inebriated when they came. 'Bang, bang, bang'. That familiar but no less frightening sound at the door. I almost spilled my drink as the sound echoed around my previously tranquil, cosy room. I looked at Mickey, he could see I was worried. Either they were here to deliver bad news, or they were here to ask me more questions. Mickey answered the door. "Good evening Sir," announced Myers as he stepped inside, followed by his blonde sidekick. Myers strode through the beige carpeted hallway and entered the living room. On seeing the empty wine bottles on the table he commented, "Having a drink are we? Miss Singer, I'm afraid tomorrow is going to be about the worst hangover of your life." He stepped towards me revealing a pair of handcuffs. "Nicole Singer, I am arresting you on suspicion of murder. You have the right to remain silent. Anything you do say can and will be used as evidence in the court of Law."

By the time he had read my rights, my hands were behind my back and cuffed tight. "I don't understand. How can you be arresting me, I'm not a murderer!" Jason stood speechless with shock. I had never seen him so still. Mickey came over to me. "We'll get you out of this. It has to be some kind of mistake!" he yelled at Myers. Dread filled my veins. What if there was no way out? I knew I was innocent but what if I'd been set up? History has shown it can happen. Life in a prison cell, I'm not sure I can cope. "Right Miss Singer, let's get you to the station. There you can tell us everything." Myers said as he led the way out of the living room and toward the front door. His sidekick forcefully placed her hand in the middle of my back and started pushing me out of my house. "Let's go." she said firmly. She was far rougher than the detective and I got the impression she liked to be in control. I turned my head to look at my house for what could've been the last time in a long time. Jason was mouthing something, *call me*.

I waited until I reached the car to cry. They shouldn't have needed to worry about me as much as they did, it was the least I could do. I had no idea what was waiting for me at the station, all I knew was that someone thought I was a murderer. I broke down, considering the possible outcome. The drive was only fifteen minutes but it felt like a lifetime to be left alone with adrenalin and what ifs. Neither Myers nor the woman made any attempt to speak to me throughout the journey. A part of me assumed they would be poking at me outside the interview for a confession, but it was almost like I wasn't there. As we drove along Derby road I remembered yesterday. Then I realized, it was the first time I had remembered the exact events of the day before. What if I had done something, would I even know? Lately it felt like I was losing it, I couldn't even remember performing simple tasks, thinking about normal things like work, washing up, watching TV. I had to consider the possibility that as crazy as it sounded, there could be more to this than I knew. Surely Jason would know, he barely leaves my side? My mind is rushing with questions, scenarios where I'm carted off to an asylum, or prison where I'll never see Jason again. I can't let that happen. They don't have proof, can they arrest me without proof?

Arriving at the police station I swallowed hard, as I saw the long grey building made up of two rectangles, one smaller than the other. It is made completely of tiny glass tiles, somewhat public. Myers eases the handbrake on. "Hannah, please escort Miss Singer while I handle the paper work," Myers ordered and sauntered into the grey building. Hannah put her hand over my head as I climbed out of the car, my legs trembling. She walked me through the main doors and after receiving a second set of commands from Myers, we continued down a lengthy corridor. The strong fluorescent strip lights made my eyes sting. They reminded me of school. The floor was a horrible grey/white tiled lino, it had the smell of old rubber and paper. Everything in this place was so depressing. As we approached the end of the corridor, Hannah unlocked a door to the right, stopped outside and held the door open for me. Reluctantly, I stepped inside the room.

"Take a seat," she said, turning on an over-sized spot lamp on the stainless steel desk. I pulled out a chair from under the table with my leg and sat down. Myers walked in. "Is there anything you would like to say before we begin Miss Singer?" "I just want to know what's going on," I sobbed. "You will, soon enough," he told me, pushing a video tape into the VCR and pressing play. Simultaneously Hannah pressed the record button on the tape player. I was reluctant to speak, knowing that everything I said could be regurgitated back to me and used against me. "Interview with N cole Singer, March thirteenth, eighteen hundred hours. Detective Myers and myself, Constable Hannah Richards are present. Showing the interviewee CCTV footage." Myers switched on the television.

A black and white picture appeared on the screen. I could see it was a multi storey car park. It was footage from a security camera. Someone was walking towards the camera from the opposite side of the car park. It was a woman. I couldn't make out any detail other than her hair and her shoes. I could tell from the beat of her walk and by the way her curly hair bounced off of her shoulders, that she was happy. Suddenly I recognized the walk. As she came closer towards the camera I could see she was smiling. I could see it was Rebecca. She took the keys from her hand bag and walked to the driver's side of her car. The lower half of her body was off screen now and all I could see was the back of her head, and that beautiful hair. A gloved black hand appeared from nowhere and grasped the back of Rebecca's head. The car window splintered as her head was thrust into the glass. Knocked unconscious she began to fall. Another gloved hand appeared and together they caught Rebecca as she slid down the side of the car. The gloved figure was wearing a black leather jacket and black leather trousers or jeans, it was difficult to tell from the black and white footage.

Rebecca was being dragged to the other side of the car. As they appeared near the boot the attacker's head came into view, it was a women. Her hair seemed to be the same length as mine, though it was black. The woman laid Rebecca on the floor and went to the boot. Opening the door, she took out some rope and pulled it taut between her hands. Coiling it neatly, she then reached inside the boot again, this time pulling out a bandana. She strutted over to Rebecca's head and knelt down. All I could see now were the attacker's boots poking out just beyond the bumper. They were both out of the shot and my mind began to wonder. Taking my eyes away from the screen briefly I looked to my right. Myers was staring at me, trying to work out if my reactions were genuine.

Noticing movement in the corner of my eye, I turned to face the screen again. Rebecca must have come around now as she reappeared, blindfolded, gagged and hands tied behind her back. The woman stood up behind her. I couldn't hear what she said as the sound was little to non-existent, but Rebecca climbed into the back seat of her car on her stomach. She wriggled like a prehistoric lizard as the woman shoved her in by her feet. She walked briskly around the car to get into the drivers' side, but as she approached the boot, she changed direction suddenly and headed straight for the camera. On reaching the lens she bent down, then stood quickly, flipping her hair away from her face. I gasped, my mouth ajar and dry. The woman in black violently stabbed out the lens with Rebecca's car key. As the lens shattered into broken shards, I saw my image through the smashed glass. Her face was distorted and wicked looking, but there was no mistaking the woman in black was me.

The television screen, now engulfed in static, hissed and buzzed, prompting me to break the eerie stillness in the room. My mind was frozen, I was paralyzed. "Where did you hide the body?" I jumped as Detective Myers' voice came in loud and sharp, breaking the concrete mould around my body. I moved my eyes to look at him, I couldn't speak but my eyes were crying innocence. I had never felt so confused or unstable. I could see that it was me on the security tape but I didn't know how or why. "Maybe it was an impostor, someone who looks like me. It's a set up, it has to be!" I screamed. The woman on the tape was so strong, so confident and forthright in her mannerisms. We looked the same but that was as far as the similarities went. I couldn't even imagine doing something like that. Admittedly I had many ideas of what I might do to Rebecca if there weren't any consequences for my actions, but I had always known it was never worth it.

For the next three hours I felt like road kill being pecked at by vultures. I was verbally battered by detective Myers. He wanted me to tell him the whereabouts of Rebecca's body. He told me they had officers scouting the woods for her body and that if I told them where she was, they could look at reducing my sentence. I swallowed hard at the word 'sentence'. A long sentence, a short sentence. Each could be equally soul destroying but there was nothing I could do to help myself, I didn't even know who I was any more. I dropped my head, feeling pitiful. Assuming this was a non verbal message from me communicating that I was not going to co-operate, Myers slammed his fist down on the table in front of my head. "Do you think we have time for you to feel sorry for yourself?!" He spat, inches away from my face. I was so segregated. I knew I had done something wrong but I couldn't explain what or why. Tears came rolling down my cheeks as I pleaded, "I'm sorry I can't tell you where she is. If I knew I would. I don't even know what happened, I don't remember anything!" Using up all the air in my lungs, I shut down, a crumpled defeated mess. I was exhausted from the emotion.

"I know where she is." I had done something bad, very bad, but I would be a worse person if I let Nicole take the fall for it. She was weak, pathetic. I did it for her, so she could sort out this mess she calls a life. Myers backed off; he could tell something was different. He stepped away and then turned to face me, looking me up and down as if he was checking I was still the same person sitting there. Myers looked at his bitch sidekick, searching for a clue of what to do next. "Would you two like some time alone?" I asked with a seductive smile. They snapped out of it and all eyes were on me, just the way I liked it. "You won't find her. That bitch's body is long gone." I snarled. "So you know where Rebecca is?" Myers asked hopefully. "No, you won't find her because she doesn't exist. Rebecca Singer does not exist!" "Are you trying to tell us you've eradicated the body?" asked Myers, with a disgusted yet intrigued expression on his face. "Why don't you call up your boys in the woods and then you can tell me?" I said playfully. "I will not continue these games; tell us what you've done with her!" Myers snapped. "Oh yes you will and I can play all night detective." I smiled. "We're keeping you in; I suggest you get yourself a lawyer- a good one." He'd had enough. Poor Myers was showing me his weakness. "Take her to a cell," Myers ordered the blonde sidekick. "Keep a close eye on her." he added. I stopped suddenly before the open door. "Get Doctor James Hammond. None of this is her fault."

That night I awoke under a musty smelling blanket on a steel bed. I had been dreaming I was eight years old again. In the comfort and the safety of my bedroom. Mum was downstairs making my packed lunch for the next day at school. Dad was calling me down for breakfast. I fell back into slumber with thoughts of my loving parents, my childhood home and hope that I could pull through. That was before Dad left and Nell became a hopeless old drunk.

When I was awoken by the sound of jingling keys I had almost forgotten where I was and why. The cell door opened and a female warden walked in. Behind her followed Mickey and Jason. Tears started streaming down my face. "Take these off please," I asked the warden, holding out my wrists. She obliged and I embraced Mickey, then Jason. I held them so tight, I never wanted to let go. "So what have you done that deserves getting banged up for the night?" Jason jested as he perched on the edge of my metal bed. He was trying to make light of the situation, typical Jason. Mickey took my hands in his and led me to the bed. I sat down with him next to Jason. He looked at me as he held my hands and asked me, "Nicki, did you do it?" I jumped up from the bed, wrenching my hands away from him. "No of course I bloody didn't!" I was starting to remember why Mickey irritated me so much, how could he doubt me? "I'm telling you guys, someone's set me up, that's the only way!" I protested.

"Miss Singer, there's someone here to see you." We all turned around to find Myers stood in the door way. Somehow the tension from last night had left his voice and he seemed to approach me differently, gently. Jason handed me a pair of trousers and a top. "Can I just change my clothes first please Detective?" I asked affably. He nodded 'yes'. "In private?" I added, gesturing towards Myers and the warden, then the door. He looked at the warden and nodded her over. "We'll be outside," he said as they closed the door. "Leather?" I said to Jason. "Yeah you know, I thought they might be more comfortable on these hard surfaces. I've spent a night or two in a foreign cell love." I smiled, Jason always remembered the details, especially when clothes were involved. "Thanks," I mustered. I hoped he knew how grateful I was, I just wasn't capable of showing it.

***

After no more than six hours sleep on a steel bed, I was still emotionally annihilated from the day before. As soon as I was dressed, the door opened and Myers's sidekick strode in. She walked towards me, never making eye contact and replaced my cuffs. *How dare she ignore me. To her I'm just another no good criminal in the unforgiving clutches of the judicial system*, I thought. "Let's go," Myers ordered, leading the way towards the door. We turned left into the same room we were in last night. *This is it*, I thought, *this is where it all comes out*. As I entered the plain white room, a silhouette changed from sitting to standing. It was James. He stood before me with his hand extended. I took it.

"What are you doing here Doctor?" I accepted the seat he offered. "Well, you asked the Detectives to bring me here. They were hoping I might be able to shed some light on this case." He sat calmly, hands cupped. "I don't know what you're talking about Doctor. I never asked them to bring you here, and I certainly don't know why my confidential records about a little mishap remembering details should have anything to do with what's going on here." I could see he was still trying to figure it out. "Detective, I'm sure I don't need to show you her files for you to see that she is clearly suffering from a mental illness." I look shocked in order to cover my identity. Detective Myers is staring at me. He beckons James over to the door. They step outside but the door is still ajar. "We don't have enough evidence to hold her here, but we certainly don't want her skipping the country any time soon. I know this woman has something to do with the disappearance but we have to let her go unless we can find proof." I can't see Myers, but I know he will be rubbing his beard as he talks. "Well, I can definitely make sure she stays somewhere that you can find her."

I didn't like the sound of this. I tried to lean in closer to the door but Hannah clocked me and slammed the door shut. Minutes later they both return. Doctor James picks up my file and looks at me with pursed lips. "Will you come easily or do I need my drugs?" "What's going on, why won't anyone tell me what's happening?" "Benzo it is then." The needle goes into my neck so fast I barely feel it. Slowly my eyes become weaker, the edges of people just blurring into the white background. I begin to fall off my chair and I am caught. I can hardly lift the weight of my head but I know that James is on my right and Myers on the other side. That bastard. How could James do this to me?

I don't know where they're taking me. The door swings open. The lights begin to fade, losing their brightness. I am being pulled down a corridor, my legs trailing out behind me. I notice how my ankles almost look dislocated. We stop at the last door in the hall, it enters into the car park at the back of the building. Just as it swings shut, I make out the blurred faces of Mickey and Jason from behind a pillar. They saw the whole thing, they will help me. They roughly shove me into the back of James' car, it smells like candy floss. I notice Jason's mini before they slam the door shut and start the engine. Myers smiles and waves as James pulls away from the police station. I have let her down and now everything I tried to protect her from is coming to her doorstep. I knew the road we were on. It led to her. I can't let them find her, I can't let them know. Any of them.

***

Diary Entry

I have no sense of time, though I have counted twenty one sunsets. I have left my room at set intervals, they make me 'exercise'. Most of the time I am angry, but at what I cannot be sure. I remember the comforts of home. I am there. The deer are so close, so tame I could reach out and brush their noses. The stag watch from afar, protected by the surrounding wall once used to entrap them. It is my haven as it theirs. I remember waking up in the stairwell, gasping for air. The oxygen is so little here that even the flies fall to the ground breathless. This is the third time this month, it is a full moon. He put my writing desk up there. I would use it to draw inspiration. I feel like a queen stood upon the very heights of my castle and he is my king. I wonder when my king will return. I remember him. It is now that my anger finds me. Sometimes it is like he is here in my room with me. His face etches into the darkness as I face another night of insomnia. I know he put me here but I don't understand why. We were in love, I am in love still. I maintain hope that one day he will return for me, one day he will call. I am Eleanor and I long to return to my castle, should it remain.

Chapter Eleven: No Man's Land

It is night. The effects of the sedatives have worn off. Hammond has let us down. He plays fast and loose with the insanity plea but he knows too much. I will co operate for now but I know I am one step ahead. Jason's lights went out back at bovine drive, he is here to help. The door opens. James is standing there with a needle in one hand and the other hand outstretched to take mine. I put my hand in his. *Yes Doctor, I trust you Doctor,* I repeat inside my head. The car park is empty, everyone has gone home. Jason's mini parks behind the main gate, hidden from the security camera and Hammond. "No more needles Doc, I'm good." I sigh. "Ah Bernadette, glad you could join me, and you are anything but good my dear." "Why am I here?" I say, exhausted. "Well, we all know this is where you belong, but you wouldn't come willingly. Now I have reason to believe that you are a danger to yourself and others, which means I'll have no problem dropping you off for a little holiday. I mean, we can't have you just wondering around cutting and pasting people's lives together, can we? This way, I know you are safe and I know where to find you." He smiles at me as though he's just solved world poverty.

Maybe he is right. Maybe I have gone about this the wrong way. I have let her down. Instead of helping her cope I have brought her here, to Rampton. Its Georgian windows are streaked with metal bars, barely big enough to see out of. The red bricks seem intrusive, glaring at me from the concrete park. There is little greenery and I wonder how they get their fresh air. Soon I will be one of them. Dosed up so much that I won't even know my own name. I can't believe I've let it come to this. "Please Jim, don't do this. Nicole is fine, you can have her, I'll leave her alone. Please don't put us here." I was shocked to hear myself begging, usually it would be something I could expect from Nicole but not me. I had no choice. Once you were in a place like this there was rarely a way out. Hammond just stared at the floor, his grasp remained on my right elbow. "I know what you are capable of Bernadette, that's why I'm putting you here. It's not fair that Nicole should be punished too, but that's just the way it is. You should have thought of that before you took Rebecca."

We have started walking to the front entrance. As we get closer, the shadows of the four-storey building towers above engulf us in their darkness. I notice a security camera in the corner of the doorway, I turn away to conceal my face. Looking over my shoulder, I can see Jason creeping up the driveway. Mickey is several metres behind him, non committal as usual. It doesn't matter, Jason and I can do this without him. I give Jason a wink, he knows what it means. In a split second I am behind James, my chained cuffs around his neck limiting the oxygen to his brain. He struggles, his hands trying to grasp underneath my wrists, flailing helplessly. I pull back hard as he coughs, his face now turning a hint of purple. "Put the keys on the floor, now," I whisper in his ear over his shoulder. I make sure he knows I mean business by tugging on the restraint a little harder. "Don't... do this Bernie!" He barely gets the words out as his breaths become shorter and weaker. "Do it!" I yell. His hands flap about near the pockets in his armani's and then the sound of a jingle towards the floor. Jason grabs the keys as I remove my arms from around Hammond's ravaged neck. He stumbles to the floor spluttering. "You won't get away with this Bernadette, I won't let you." He is rubbing himself as if he is suffering from a sore throat.

"Why shouldn't I? She gets away with everything, even when she's taking from you right under your noses. Well it's time a little justice was served, don't you think?" I'm standing over him out of the camera's view. "Are you talking about Rebecca? You know where she is don't you?" He tries to stand up so I kick him back down. "It doesn't matter. You will only find her when I want you to find her, and if you're lucky she'll still be alive!" Jason is running behind me now as we hurry to the mini. We pass Mickey on the way, loitering by the gate watching, on the fence as always. It takes him a few seconds to realise that we're leaving, he looks as though he is glued to the pillar he's been hiding behind. "Are you two just going to leave him there like that?" he asks, peering in through the open back door. I disregard his question and replace it with another. "It's a long walk back to town, are you coming or what?" He shakes his head avidly and takes what feels like an hour to get inside Jason's tiny car. Jason makes a U turn and floors it through the open iron gates.

I can hear sounds. They are calling to me outside. They are

channeling toward me from the darkness. At first I am scared, I am so high. I remember how I was scared then too, at the top of my castle. But there are no deer any more, not here. It is not deer that echo sounds beyond the walls of my room. I hear her name, could it be my princess? I remember her face, she is real. I leave my bed on tiptoes, if I am disturbed they too will likely be disturbed. It is five paces to the window of my cage, five paces to see her face. I see her face, a pale skin reflecting the moon. She is angry like me but she is not Rebecca. She is not my princess, she is Bernadette.

He was making his way back to the Yellow House B&B to think about what he might do. They had dined at the Rose Garden for hours while they talked. It reminded him of Nell. She was late for work on the day they first met. He wondered if she would be there.

Henry was a very private man but he had thought that finally being able to divulge the heavy secrets of the past with his daughter might feel different to this. He expected relief, sadness on her part or perhaps even for her to be overwhelmed somewhat; but she just kept asking so many questions. He would expect questions; yes, he was prepared for those, but not quite the questions that she was asking. He knew from the many years of writing to Nicole that she should know the answers to most of the questions she was asking him. Nicole would know how much Wollaton was worth, she would know that Henry worked as an architect there and she would know its history. It may well have been that she was just so overwhelmed that she had become awestruck and lost her thoughts temporarily, but Henry was a cautious man and always tried to follow his instinct. Today, his instinct was telling him that this woman wasn't who she claimed to be. Instead of alarming her and causing a scene, he plays along with it until they manage to stop the auction. The press have arrived and they want a shot of Henry and his daughter reunited, they are asking if she will be heiress to the property, to which Henry nods and smiles. But his thoughts are centred on doing this right. He cannot return home until he is sure Nicole knows the truth, and that she will get what is rightfully hers. He poses earnestly for the photographer as she slips her arm through his. After she is gone he will call her. She is the only person that will be able to help him, even though twenty five years ago he broke her heart and she still doesn't know the truth. If he is to find Nicole he will first have to break it all over again.

Chapter Twelve: True Colours

It would be a long drive to the drop off point and we needed to avoid the city. Mickey was so quiet, just staring blankly at the road ahead through the gap between the front seats. "I saw everything you know, you're not the person I thought you were Nicole." He said without moving his gaze. Nicole, she is his friend. No matter what I think of him, he means something to her. His disappointment in me struck a chord but I didn't know how to respond. My heart ached for all of the trouble I had caused, and the damage I was about to incur, but I couldn't show any weakness, not now. We had come too far, there were too many burned bridges for repentance.

"Mickey, I don't expect you to understand what Jason and I are doing. I don't expect you to support what I have done to James or what I am about to do to Rebecca. As Nicole's friend I ask that you let it play out, and at the end if you think we deserve to be punished then I will understand. Please know this." I turn to look him in the eyes, his face is barely inches away from mine and I see he has the most forest-green eyes I have ever seen. I can't believe I haven't noticed them before. "Nicole is very ill. I am Bernadette, a creation, giving her the means to do things that she could never even dream of. To allow her this will mean the end to a miserable life for her. Without me she will remain a shadow, a faceless entity in a world filled with sunshine and trauma that she would never normally be a part of." I look deep into his eyes. His lips are pursed and his brow furrowed. He does not know me, he does not know if I am truthful and Mickey is struggling to know what is real and what could easily be some weird dream. "Without me she won't experience anything, no sorrow or joy. She is merely surviving, is that what you want for her?"

"I don't want to be a part of whatever sick game it is that you're playing. I miss my friend. My gentle, beautiful, loving friend. How can you damage her in this way, how can you possibly think you're helping?" His eyes well up as he looks to the floor. I never realised how much he cared. For someone who I thought was so shallow... He actually cared for her. "Stop the car." Mickey says firmly, his hand already on the door. Jason turns to me and I nod ok. Mickey's moral compass has had the shattering of a lifetime, but given the way he feels about her I'm quietly confident that he won't go to the police. He takes me by the chin swiftly and pulls my gaze toward him. "When this is over you have me to answer to, and if Nicole is hurt in any way I will give you to Hammond myself." He swiftly ducks out of the car and closes the door behind him, resting his hand against the window before walking down the winding path toward Nottingham. His hands are in his front pockets but I can see from the material that they are clenched into fists. He watches his feet as he fades into a nearby corner in the road.

Ever since I'd known him he was always trying to do the right thing. I hated that. I still couldn't see what Nicole saw in him and believe me, I'd looked. Mickey's words were ringing in my ears, never in the time I had known Nicole had I been aware of such consequences. What if it does all go wrong? It wouldn't be Jason who was accountable, just me. Except it isn't just me, it's her, the person I'm doing all of this for. It's for Nicki. Now that James is aware of what we are doing, I don't have as much time as I had planned. I still don't know what would become of Rebecca. I don't know what I plan to do if she resists my questioning. Should I kill her? Would I be just in my cause or would people think I was just like her? That was possibly the worst scenario, for people to think I am like her. Nicole is weak, she could never do what I am about to do. I am trying to envision how it will play out and we haven't even made it to the drop point yet. Not far now.

It is pitch black, no guiding lights here, but Bernie seems to be doing ok. Mickey has just left, I don't think she's worried about the fall out, after all it is her that he has fallen out with, not Nicole. She knows Mickey would do anything for Nicki and given that he knows so little about her condition, he's not about to interfere. At least I hope not. In some ways I wish it was daylight. The journey from Retford to Nottingham is a beautiful one but it is going unappreciated in the darkness. We are surrounded by rolling hills, grass of all colours, yellow, green, red. The poppies will be gone soon, their petals will blow away in the breeze like all the other autumn leaves. Such beauty, in a few months people will forget what it looked like and they will see a picture of death. The hills will look vacant and wild, clumpy soil turned by the farmer and his tractor. The bliss from seeing a field of red poppies will be a distant memory, and we will be left with bitter frost and dried twigs. We are driving to Bilborough park. On the outskirts of the park I left the rented van with Rebecca in the back. She should still be unconscious from the chloroform. If she isn't we could be in for some trouble. Rebecca could be rocking that van back and forth right now, drawing all kinds of attention. They would run to her rescue, like they always do. Bernie and I are the only ones who see through her, I don't understand how that is. God I hope she is silent, but most of all I hope we get away with this.

Chingford Road takes us through a built up residential area. I think of all the families sleeping, not knowing of the shocking events that are about to take place, not even in their wildest dreams. I have hidden the van behind a couple of warehouses, opposite the sports centre on Calveley Road. We have been driving for just over fifty minutes, with so little traffic on the roads we have cut our journey time by over twenty minutes. It is still pitch black, we have been travelling without any lights since entering Chingford Road, but I can just make out the warehouse as we drive across the park. Bernie cuts the engine and removes the keys from the ignition, the little mini rattles as it shuts down. I grab our torches from the glove box and step onto the sodden parkland. Shining my torch around the corner, I can see the white van, standing alone beside the disused warehouse. There is stillness. We are on the outskirts of Nottingham, peaceful, without the hum drum of city life whirring in the background, even at three in the morning. We approach the van with caution, so as to not alert Rebecca if she happens to be conscious. I find my other set of keys and release the back doors.

She is lying on her side, her hands are fastened with a cable tie and the gag remains in her mouth, just as I left her. She almost looks peaceful. She has been in our care for four days already. After Bernie apprehended her at the car park we had to leave a day between meeting to avoid suspicion. First we had to be sure that no-one would report her missing after twenty four hours. Of course the major didn't, he was quite happy for the public to see Rebecca entering his house and staying there, but to admit to them that he was worried about her safety by reporting her missing was a completely different page. He was more than happy for the public to see him as the local hero, giving his home to a woman in need, but to hint that there was something more between them, that he was getting something out of it, would be disastrous for his image.

She was still breathing but it seemed the effects of the chloroform were beginning to wear off. Her feet began to twitch and her fingers curled behind her back. I looked at Bernie. Without saying a word she slammed the doors shut and climbed into the passenger's seat. "You're in charge of the van" she said and jumped back into the mini.

We take the van twenty minutes outside of Nottingham City to a forest. Parts of it are open to the public but there is a back entrance hidden from view. I slow the van to crawling pace. Ideally I would have turned the lights off, but there is no way we'd find the place in complete darkness. "Look for a gap in the hedge," I tell Bernadette over the transceiver. She winds her window down, bobbing and weaving her head as the torch searches over the hedgerows. "Found it." I pull up the van by the roadside. The next part would be tricky. We had to make sure the entrance stayed hidden. Bernie held the torch while I cut the fence at either side of two posts. We stamped it down to the floor leaving just enough room for the van to get through. Bernie started up the van and drove it over the forest mound, twigs and bits of hedge snapping as they succumbed to the weight of the rent-o-van. After she was clear I began rebuilding the fence. The hedge wasn't so easy to repair, but I pushed it up to the height of the hedge as best as I could. I jumped back into the driver's seat and we made our way to the derelict warehouse that awaited Rebecca.

One more dose of chloroform would give us until tomorrow afternoon. She gagged a little as we sent her under with the toxic gas, it was obviously hurting her body but there wasn't any other choice. She would not swallow sleeping pills, and short of hitting her in the head every time, we were at a stalemate with this particular solution. For now Rebecca would remain concealed in the van, behind the warehouse. "Are you sure you want to come back to this tomorrow?" I asked Bernadette. "As sure as I'll still be alive tomorrow," she smiled, opening the doors to the mini. We were both exhausted and still had work ahead of us tomorrow. Thirty minutes and we would be back home, safe. We had pulled it off.

Chapter Thirteen: The Reckoning

Every Wednesday it came through the letter box like a brick. It was the Nottingham local newspaper. Most days she would approach it with the usual envy and disgust, it was far more difficult to shut out the world when it landed on your welcome mat every week. Today was different, today she saw his face.

There he was, a blast from the past, smack bang on the front of her paper, in her house once more. He'd left without saying and now he'd arrived without saying. Why was he back? She wondered if it had anything to do with the message he had left for Nicole. Had Nicole been to see him? Nell wondered if it was even her place to care anymore. Ever since she had told Nicole it was like she had become someone else; cold, distant, protective and secretive. Nell knew she had lost her as soon as the words had left her mouth. She doesn't want to pick it up, but curiosity had the better of her as soon as she had seen his face. Had he come back for her? It seemed there were two stories here. "Nicole and Henry Middleton reunite to stop sale of Hall."

***

Henry Middleton had been a changed man for nearly a year. They were supposed to getting married tomorrow but it was not out of interest in their wedding venue that he visited the County Court today, no, Henry Middleton was saying

Goodbye.

The building was dreary and typically modern British architecture. He much preferred the older end of Nottingham, the parts that had steadied among the growing city. He was able to compromise on some of it, after all he was aware that all things need to adapt and grow with the times, he knew that better than anyone. He thought about his baby girl. She would be a year old tomorrow and Henry would not be there. He would not be there to see her master walking, he would not witness her using the potty, he would miss her calling him Da Da and would never hear her say "I love you." He didn't know if he would ever see her again but in truth it would be less painful if he didn't. She had begun to reflect the beauty of her Mother more and more with each day that passed. With each look she gave there came a jolt to his heart with the power of fifty volts. The older she got the worse it became.

Nell had no idea what he was thinking, what with all that he had left behind to be with her. It was chance that they had met and at first Henry had not seen it as anything serious, not really anything more than a distraction from her. For a while it had worked, but Henry found himself spending more and more time by her side. He would see her at work, sitting at the same table reading the paper for several hours while she poured him coffee and joined him on her lunch break. They dated for three months before she asked him to move in with her, six months later his baby girl arrived. He thought that living with someone again might act as a barricade to his thoughts, his emotions, but he couldn't seem to fall in love with Nell no matter how hard he tried. Henry knew that his emotional strings were still tied to Eleanor, and if he were ever to move on completely he would have to cut them.

The two large flagstone steps would be the first hurdle he had to cross. He stepped in knowing that when he came out, he would be a changed man. Would his daughter ever forgive him? He didn't know and struggled to care a little for anyone else, as he was barely able to surface for breath under the sea of depression he had been in since that day eight years ago. He had not received any medical help for his condition. He had not visited the doctor when it happened, in fear of being institutionalized, but research into depression had fluctuated in the eighties and Henry had been diagnosed and treated. On his first visit he had asked young Doctor Evan if there was a cure for a broken heart, to which he had replied "no, no cure, but these meds will certainly help take the edge off," and passed Henry his prescription. From then on it had been difficult for Henry to distinguish dream from reality, and he would wake part way through a vivid dream, believing in the lucidity of it all.

Perhaps that's why he felt as though all of this today was happening to someone else and he was just watching it from the outside. Maybe that's why the consequences didn't seem real. Either way he had to go through with it. He would be beginning a new life while Nell struggled to raise their daughter alone. He had already begun the process when he met Nell, introducing himself under a different name had given him an adrenalin rush, the first sense of being alive he had felt in years. It was his decision never to tell her the truth. If Nell were to discover his past there was a chance it would ruin their future and Henry was desperately trying to hold onto any hope of forgetting where he had come from. He couldn't do it if Nell knew the truth. He hoped that she would never realise that she had been little more than a scapegoat to help Henry escape from his twisted and tortured past.

***

I felt like an idiot. I felt like a fool for not knowing. What kind of person doesn't know their history? Anger is building as I realise I look like a fool. I hate looking a fool. I have to see for myself. I must know the truth, for her.

The door opens after the third set of knocks. Is she going to be hammered as usual? The door releases a little, it is still on the chain. "Nell it's me Nicole, I need to talk to you." I can hear her fiddling with the rusting old chain behind the door. "What do you want? I've said everything I want to say to you." I'm despondent but I eventually say, "I need some answers Nell, about Dad, I mean Jeffery." The door swings open and she takes a step back. I walk in with the knowledge that Rebecca may have been right. There's a weight on me. If Nicole ever finds out any of this it could be the end of her.

"Jeffery isn't your father," she says, making her way back

to the kitchen. She sits down at the table. She kicks a chair out from under the table for me to sit down and slides the newspaper she's been reading across the table. "There he is," she says, a certain sadness in her eyes. They have turned dull and weak. Nell doesn't have any tears left though, she is empty. "This is him?" Nell nods, a blankness filling her eyes. "Why is he with her?" I almost shout. Just seeing her face gets my back up. "It says she's his daughter, his real daughter." "That's Rebecca, how can she be his daughter?" She is shaking her head, "I know that man as Jeffery Singer, not Henry Middleton. I'm not sure how much I can help Nicole, I'm still trying to figure it out myself." She exhales deeply, perplexed by Jeffery's sudden appearance and going by a different name. "I don't understand," I say. I'm aware that I'm not doing a very good job of staying in character but fortunately for me, Nell is completely preoccupied with the sudden appearance of her ex fiancé, my adoptive father.

I needed to know what Rebecca had to do with Wollaton. I knew for a fact that the man she stood beside in the headlines was not her father, unless there was an even darker, more twisted and evil plot behind Rebecca's upbringing. Everyone east of Beeston knew that Rebecca's Dad was a gambler, a thief. I couldn't be sure but every gut instinct I had told me that this had everything to do with money. It always had something to do with money when Rebecca was involved.

I should be going back to work today, I thought this would

be over by now, one way or another. It is going to look suspicious when Rebecca is reported missing and Nicole hasn't been to work for a week, the exact week that Rebecca has been missing. I call up Jen. I tell her I'm sick and that I won't be in for a few days, it's viral. "Are you ok Nicki?" She sounds worried and is probably referring to Nicole's meltdown from a month ago. "Yeah honestly it's just a bug, I'll be fine," I lie. The truth is I like Jen but there's a huge difference between liking someone and trusting them. There are few people that would understand the situation I'm in, few people that would take a stand against injustice, and very few who would understand my actions.

I know I need to finish what I started but I have lost momentum. This began as a lesson, I had a lesson to teach and Rebecca was the student. Now it is personal. Now I see that she has been sabotaging me, personally picking on me and my family. All of the other issues will be pushed to one side as I try to find out what she's been up to. I have to get back to her, I have to end this.

The forty five minute drive up to Clipstone was agonizing. Thoughts about what I would say whirred through my mind without focus. Every time I land on a good one, the prick in the Ford Ka in front of me slams his breaks on or decides to do twenty in a fifty zone. By the time I arrive I am even more stressed and angry, the headache seems to be lasting days. I drive the Land Rover over the threshold and get out to fix the fence. It is quiet here. The floor is lined with an array of oranges, browns and reds and I take peace in the quiet respite of the forest. Getting back in the Land Rover, I realise what I have known all along. Rebecca is not going to speak easy, she needs some persuasion. I quickly drive around to the side of the warehouse and run to the other where Rebecca is. It is silent. I unlock the van doors, she lifts her bagged head, not knowing if it's night or day. I untie her legs. "Don't try to kick me, if you do I will cut your artery and I will leave you out here to die. Do you understand me?" "Yes." her voice trembles. Once the rope is released, I grab her under the arm and help her to stand. Her hands are still tied together at the wrist and she cannot see anything but blackness.

As she stands there is a shadow mocking her movements. Jason is staring at me from inside the van, I didn't realise he was here. "Where's the car?" I ask, I hadn't noticed it when I parked the Land Rover. "It's inside." he says sternly. It is obvious he has been here for several hours, brooding. I'm wondering what may have happened if I hadn't have arrived when I did. I can't ask him what he's been doing in front of Rebecca, I can't undermine the project. I tell her we are moving to somewhere more comfortable, where she will have a chair to sit on, but that first we need to get her out of the van. "Count three paces forward," I say, letting go of her. I know it's safe to let go of her. Even if she did try to run she can't get to anywhere or anyone very quickly, but I know she won't. For all she knows there could be a wall directly in front of her, or even a hole in the floor. She had to put her trust in me. She had to listen to me and do as I told her. She walks in tiny steps, three and then stops. She is almost at the edge of the van where the doors are open to the sides. It takes every inch of restraint I have not to push her violently off the edge.

As I walk past her, she spins around and nearly falls over. "Did I tell you to move?" I shout. She turns to face the direction of my voice again, I am standing on the floor outside. The ground is muddy. Autumn leaves have been falling for a month now and they are beginning to mulch into the ground like soggy newspaper. "Jump down, it's about half a metre to the floor." As her feet leave the van floor she stumbles, her left foot catches the step and she falls. Rebecca is lying face down in the mud and I am standing. I think about how many people would want to see this, Jason included. If it were any other circumstance I would be laughing but the truth is none of this is amusing. Jason jumps down behind her from the van. He is smiling and enjoying looking down at her from above. He enjoys seeing her as the lowly snake that she is, crawling on her belly, prohibited from walking on two legs like decent folk. I am sickened by the woman who lies before me and I'm losing patience. She starts whimpering, signaling that she is hurt. Noticing the way in which she has fallen it's quite possible she may have bruised or even fractured her collarbone, a small price to pay for what she's done. "Get up!" She is the prisoner and I am the guard. Next we go inside.

The air is cold and damp. The tin roof is not sealed and there is water dripping down onto the concrete floor. It gathers in shallow pools around the large room, it ripples with the draft entering through the cracks in the iron panels. There is a single wooden chair in the centre of the room. We enter through the main door which is to the bottom right. The wind has picked up and it's now howling through the gaps in the metal sheeting. I struggle to get the massive doors shut. There is a small part of me that wants to delay closing the door. I know that the next time I walk out of here I will be a different person, maybe even a murderer. Does Rebecca know how serious I am? She should. I walk her over to her chair. "Sit down. This will be your home until you have told me everything I need to know. Unlike everyone else I can tell when you're lying, so don't even waste your breath." She starts to sob again. "Remember, out here time is precious. One night will be uncomfortable, two nights will be unfavourable, but three nights? You're looking at possible hypothermia and failure to your circulatory system so it's easier for everyone if you just answer truthfully."

"I don't understand why you've brought me here, what can I have possibly done to you to make you hate me so much?" Rebecca is still wearing the bag over her head and she isn't aware of where I'm standing. When she speaks, her head moves from side to side like a python stalking a mouse. "I know we work together but that's all I know about you."

"Ok, let's start from the beginning shall we? We first met at work. You were rude as usual. You steal, manipulate and sabotage, is that a good enough reason for me to bring you here?"

"What do you mean, sabotage?" She asks innocently. I have to calm down but I know that all of this is just a distraction, a means of 'getting to know the enemy' so that she can break me down gradually without me noticing. She forgets that I have not lived a sheltered life, I do not scam easily and where Rebecca is concerned, I refuse to give up. As there is no threat of her achieving what she intends, I decide to humour her. "I mean stealing the job that wasn't yours, a quiet whisper here, a little nudge there; how many people did you sleep with to get that job by the way?" I am leaning towards her, had she not been covered by the bag I would have been breathing in her face. Her head drops to the floor and she is still. The sobbing begins again, but this time it is different, as though she doesn't want to cry. I temporarily panic; this is the sort of thing that alerts Nicole. If she is exposed to any kind of emotion while I'm with her, it's twice as hard to lock her back down. I was thinking about damage control when....

"I don't even remember how it happened. It was so awful. I woke up and he was just there, thrusting. I thought maybe I had been drinking, I do that sometimes, to forget but I couldn't taste any alcohol. He saw the look on my face and said that if I didn't start enjoying myself he would retract his offer. So I just lay there. I don't even know if it was real, I don't even remember what happened next. All I know is that when I went to work the next day I had been promoted to floor manager. It's not my fault Nicole, I swear," she sobbed. She had made herself smaller somehow, it was as though her bones had slowly folded in on themselves and she had collapsed into a smaller frame.

She didn't believe it. In fact it was rare that anything coming out of Rebecca's mouth was truthful, unless it was guaranteed to get her something. "Is this how you persuaded someone to burn down your house? Forever playing the broken damsel aren't we Rebecca, well I'm telling you now it won't work on me!" I rip the bag from her head but she does not move. She is not listening. She has gone into her mind but she seems shocked, her ice blue eyes searching from left to right, filling with tears. "My house burnt down?" she murmurs, "how?" Jason can see that my patience is breaking; he knows I've lost my rhythm and steps forward. "You did it, everyone knows that so don't bother trying to convince us otherwise." It may be time to start proving in other ways that she means business.

She steps outside to collect the weapons and gather her thoughts; she is ever so vaguely tickled by the prospect of a pair of tweezers being used as a weapon. She had no other choice than to bring items from home; a plastic dish, a razor and clippers, a thick blanket, bleach, acid, a kitchen knife and of course, Nicole's tweezers. Slowly checking all of the items and checking the imaginary boxes they sat next to in her mind helped her feel as though she'd had enough time to reflect, but she knew if she came away for too long the effect of what was happening would wear off bit by bit and the methods of extraction needed would be venturing more and more towards the loss of life. Yes she wanted the truth but at what cost? She knew she had already put Nicole at huge risk and although she had been careful to cover her tracks she had to consider the possibility that one day she may not be around to protect Nicole from the truth. If Nicole were ever to discover what she had done it was likely she would actually turn herself in. What she was about to decide could be the difference between serving ten years and life in prison. She had to ask herself, was it really worth it?

She had been outside with the van for almost twenty minutes, staring at the empty space on the floor. Despite her altercation with the law she had not seen any police in the woods. Bernadette was smart. She knew that out of the 1045 acres of wood, her torture scene was the smallest and almost off the grid. She knew that even if they located it on a map it was highly unlikely they would be able to access it. It used to be a storage facility for fireworks, and before that it had belonged to a timber company. Fifteen years ago the National Trust stopped all cutting of trees in Sherwood Forest and the warehouse was left abandoned. In more recent years the carnival committee were using it as a storage space for fireworks, among other crap, until the National Trust quashed that too. They said the fireworks were detrimental to the health and habitats of the local wildlife, the noise scared them and the litter they left in their wake was not acceptable. Thanks to them, she now had the perfect place to carry out her plan completely under the radar. After collecting her thoughts, she turned to head back in. She stops just short of the door. She knows if she enters the warehouse it is going to turn ugly. She may have to do things that she doesn't want to do, but she is not one to back down or walk away from unfinished business. Her hands feel the cold as she grasps the sturdy iron door and hauls it open.

"Why are you doing this to me? I've never done anything to you!" She looked like a little rag doll, frail and limp perched on the insignificant wooden chair. Jason had been busy while I was outside. "Just think of me as a spokesperson for the collective." I smiled. Sensing I was back in the room, Rebecca tried reasoning with me. "Please Nicole. I know you're better than this, you have to let me go." She was desperately trying to wriggle out of the rope Jason had tied around her neck and hands. "I don't have to do anything! I'm here because no-one else has the balls to do what's right. I'm here to make sure you get what you deserve. You're right about one thing though, Nicole is better than this. She's better than you and half the people in this city. That's why I'm here, to get the job done." If Rebecca was trying to appeal to my better side she needn't have bothered. I had left any feelings of sympathy or understanding outside with the van, and with this new sense of freedom, it was only a matter of time before I completely lost control. I hoped my lack of humanity was only temporary, it could mean the difference between ten years and life in prison, should I be caught. "I don't understand. Why are you talking about Nicole that way? You are Nicki." Rebecca was confused and disorientated by her surroundings. "Nicki's not here right now!" I yelled in her face. I was enjoying this. "So you can save your tears for someone who gives a crap!" I scorned. She was scared, very scared; tears rolling down along those perfectly defined cheek bones and onto her white mud stained shirt.

Chapter Fourteen: Shadows Of The Past

It is her twenty sixth year now. Twenty six years to reply to the man she loved and lost. It had been so hard for her to reply. It would be like admitting that she was not a part of the world any more. Mac had sent her photographs of Rebecca, she was beautiful. He told Eleanor that she was wonderfully intelligent in the same sentence as asking her to finance Rebecca's education at Lady Bay Primary. He had it all planned. It was his intention to put Rebecca in an all girls' school at the age of eleven. He explained to Eleanor that if he was to undo Rebecca's unfair start in life, they needed to provide her with the very best in education. She knew he was right, and Eleanor would do anything to give her little girl everything she deserved.

She was feeling particularly strange today. The doctor had told her that it was unnatural to feel a sense of loss. Eleanor knew that this was more than her usual feelings of loneliness and bereavement. On the day they took her she promised she would do it for herself and to protect her babies. Rebecca would have been seven years old then. She had known that no matter how much she loved them and wanted to be a part of them, that she would bring nothing more than sadness. Without Henry by her side she was empty and powerless to give of herself to them. She knew that she would never live on the outside again, and at first, whenever she thought of this, it killed her a little more than it had before.

Today, and for the last five years, she had known that she would never get out. Hope was something she only kept for other people but Eleanor lived somewhere that hope did not see. In writing to Henry, she was merely hoping to see if he was still alive, that he hadn't forgotten her and perhaps he may even see fit to tell her of their baby girl. She wanted to know everything about her and felt shame when she thought about how her baby might know of her. Only a terrible mother would leave their baby alone. She knew that Henry would look after her though. He was not like other men. He was loving and kind, firm but fair, and it weakened her when she thought how she had ruined the chance for them to raise a family together. It was only the past that was stopping Eleanor from getting better.

She is holding Henry's letter. He writes to apologize for being unable to stay by her side. He says he wished he could have helped her, perhaps if he had tried harder then she would not be at Rampton. He spoke of love, said he would always love her, though his recent actions would not give this impression. In the other hand she held a letter from Mac and a picture of her. 'Rebecca, eight years old,' it read. Henry had not told her anything of the baby, only that she would be looked after. Now, after nearly twenty years, she wants to know what happened to her baby. In here she is being chased by the shadows of the past, memories serve as constant reminders that she was a terrible mother, abandoning her children.

Doctor Lewis disagreed. He told Eleanor that she had done the necessary thing, the only thing she could have done protect her family and her status. But she had seen the newspapers. They did not report that she was a mother who was doing the best thing for her children; they likened her to a actions to those of a crazed psychopath, who lies and cheats for their own amusement. Reading the story did not hurt her though. The pain she felt from losing Henry and knowing that she would never be a mother to her children pained her more than anything, and acted as a barrier to all other pains. It was true, Eleanor was numb to anything else. She even remembered the day her taste returned. It was thirty days after she was first committed that her ability to taste food came back, she realized she had taken many things in life for granted. Her window is so small she can see very little out, but she remembers hearing the voice of her daughter.

When she had finally caught a glimpse of the woman she knew instantly that it was not her, but the voice, the voice she could not forget. It had started her thinking. She had always wondered what had become of them, all the while knowing that she would never be a part of their lives, not really. It must be such an awful reality for them, to know that their mother resided in a mental institution. She is looking to the window from her bed, imagining she is looking at the deer, pretending she is home. What will she write? After all these years will he even remember her, will he still be there? She cannot hide any longer, it is time that Eleanor Middleton became a part of the world again.

***

She had been up and dressed at six a.m. Nell Singer had not been able to sleep since the reappearance of her ex fiancé. Nor had she been able to cope in her usual way, she wouldn't find the answers to her questions at the bottom of a bottle. It had taken her eighteen years to even think about healing her wounds, to even approach the reasons why. This time, the bottle could only hinder her from discovering the answers. Where had he been, what had he been doing, why did he leave without even saying goodbye? Mostly that was what made her drink, constantly wondering if she could have saved them if she had known he was going, but he hadn't given her that chance. The post arrived at eight thirty. In the two hours she had been up previously, she had made the bed, swept and mopped the floor, dusted and hovered and made breakfast. Now she was watching This Morning, (she had built a love affair with Philip Schofield since she kicked the drink).

Thumbing through it she saw a hand-written envelope, it was addressed to Henry. She stood still at the door, analysing the writing. She did not recognise it. Whoever it was obviously hadn't been in contact with Henry since before he left, otherwise they would have known he no longer resided here. Nell was not usually a rule breaker but curiosity had the better of her already. If Henry wasn't going to offer her an explanation then she would just have to discover her own truth, and there was a chance that this could help. She tore through the envelope like it was tracing paper.

She reads;

My Dearest Henry, please forgive me for taking such a lengthy period to reply, I have been somewhat detached from the outside world and time has almost slipped away from me without notice. It seems I am always asking this of you Henry, for your forgiveness. I feel it is something that I will never have since you never did come back to me.

I have felt the pull again lately. In here I am nothing but a single woman but in my body and spirit I am a Mother, a carer to two children and I cannot, nor do I ever want to forget them. I knew you would give her a good life Henry, that you would protect her from all the mistakes I made. The doctor says I must be patient Henry, but I fear if I am not improved in nearly twenty years then I shall never see the person I once was. If only I could see her Henry. I wonder what you named her? How did you cope with the womanly aspects of her teenage years, I hope you didn't fight too much. If you did, please know that it is sometimes beyond a woman's reach to control their outbursts, but I know your gentle heart would have put her fire out.

I did not tell the press anything. They kept coming around like hungry vultures and it was all I could do not to scream and cry in their presence. They were so noisy outside my window, shouting and jeering until the nurses threatened to call the police. I prayed and prayed until they clambered back into their vans, I didn't want to draw attention after everything we had been through.

I write now because it is only now that I realise I will not make it out of here. The doctor says I must continue to be hopeful but with each dawn it is not hope I feel but another lonesome twenty four hours without my family. I am so envious of you darling. You have been able to watch her grow into a woman, our child. I was supposed to get better and find you, it was never meant to be this way and every day the remorse I feel makes me weak. I would like to see her Henry, just once. I know not what you have told her about her Mother but it matters not. I just want to see her, she is part of us both and she is proof that I have left something of beauty in the world. Everything here is so bleak and colourless and I long to feel love, a connection. Please bring her to me Henry, I don't know how much longer I can stay.

All my love

Eleanor.

She is standing on the spot by her pink letter box, she does not notice the draught pouring in. Her brain is in overload, questions firing off one after the other before she has time to find an answer for any of them. The man in the paper was definitely Jeffery, which meant that Jeffery was definitely Henry, he must have changed his name to get away from the press she thought. This wasn't some far off fantasy she was reading about, Nell actually remembered some of when this happened. She had never seen anything in the papers, but in her line of work, local tongues were often closer to the truth than the press. Of course, Nell hadn't realised that it was Jeffery that they were referring to....

Slowly she was beginning to piece together the broken pieces of Jeffery's past. Eleanor it seems was the mother of a child they had together, but who, she wondered. Nearly twenty years is what she said, that's around the time Nell had first met Jeffery. Her face began to drop as the truth started to unfold in her mind. Did he run away to be with her? No, she said she hasn't seen him twenty years. Were they married? Was he still married to her when he left, could that be why he wouldn't or couldn't marry Nell? There were too many questions and some things were just too unclear. She would not let it break her heart before she knew the facts.

***

"How do you know the man you're standing with in the

paper?" I ripped the brown sack from her head. I wanted to know how she was planning on ripping Nicole's life apart this time. I walked over to the far side of the room. The label read 'highly corrosive'. I smiled as I carried the large container over to Rebecca, ensuring the label was visible to her. She squinted and blinked, her mind reeling from the sudden realization of her surroundings. Turning her head left and right, Rebecca took in the large empty room, it was apparent she had no idea where she was. "So, what parts of you are actually real?" She sniffled as I probed her. I wanted to take everything away from her, everything that she had drawn upon to get ahead. Nicole was such a good girl, always being knocked down by people like Rebecca who refuse to play by the rules. That's why I'm here. As far Rebecca is concerned, I've thrown away the rule book and I'm certainly not afraid to get my hands dirty. Someone has got to stop this beast.

"I know your beautiful hair isn't. Is there anything about you that hasn't been soiled by lies and deceit?" She looked pathetic. "Don't tell me, you're the last great innocent Rebecca. That's the problem with people like you, it's always someone else's fault, isn't it?" With that I pour acid onto her crowning glory. She whimpers as it sizzles in to her scalp. She throws her head back, screaming in agony as I drip small amounts along her slender thighs. I part her legs violently and let the acid run down her inner thigh to form a deadly pool beneath her. I stood back, ensuring I had a satisfactory view of her squirming. Jay held her firmly by the shoulders as she tried to writhe away from the lethal fluid. "That's for Stan," Jay whispered in her ear as locks of gold started to fall to the floor, eaten away and corroded, the golden roots now stained blood red.

Jason was getting his revenge and he deserved it. We had planned this attack months ago. He had pleaded with Nicole to unite with him, begging her to look deep within herself and recognize her need for retribution. She knew it was beyond her, but Bernadette had heard his call and came running to the sound of justice being served. The idea of Nicole finally rising up to take what was hers, to push her enemies aside was one that Bernadette couldn't resist. For Jay it was a different revenge. Rebecca had hurt him in the most powerful way that anyone could, and he would never forget the pain of losing his lover. He had to avenge Stan. He had been a good man but once again Rebecca had used her charm to steal from us.

Stan had made it easy for Jason to come out. Everything is easier when you're in love. They had made plans, a future together. For months they soared miles above the city in their bubble. Then Rebecca interfered. Stanley had strayed one night, in a moment of temporary confusion Rebecca had pounced. He and Jay had been fighting. Jason was in a whirlwind romance, something he'd been craving for what felt like a lifetime. He wanted to express his love freely, to everyone. Stan's fear of rejection would not allow it. He was too subdued by what people might think (Stan had many admirers, many of them women). Only one of those women knew him well, Rebecca. There she was, on the end of the phone when he needed a friend. But she did the dirty. She waited until he was vulnerable, then made her move.

On the night of his emotional down fall they had met at a bar down town called Twisters. It was a sleaze bar but neither of them cared for what was there. It was merely a place where they could each speak freely. After many shots, chasers and caring words, Rebecca escorted Stan to her house. She had persuaded Stan it would be better for him not to see Jay in his drunken state, pretending she cared whether or not Stan would fuel another argument with Jay. In the eyes of the law, what Rebecca did would be considered as rape, but Stan was too naïve and too much of a gentleman to ever accuse her of something so intentionally vile. The day after, he told Jason the exact details of what had happened; that he couldn't remember much, only that he had awoken naked and in bed with Rebecca, who was also naked. Whilst she cuddled in to his chest she had voiced her gratitude to Stan for being such a gentle lover, but also her concern for their friendship, that it may be threatened by their hasty consummation. Stan had spoken to her clearly and with care when he promised her it would not jeopardize their bond, but that he was in love with Jay. He bled his heart out, stating how he'd been stupid not to believe in his partnership with Jason. That's when she turned bitter. At that point he apologized, expressed his regret further and left.

Stan returned home, telling Jason everything. They worked together. They were in love. For a while Jay thought forgiving Stan was easy, everything fell into place like nothing had really happened, after all Jason knew that Stan was gay. There was absolutely no way that he could have slept with Rebecca, which angered him more. The fact that she would make up something like that just reeked of desperation and jealousy. Jason was right. While he and Stan pieced their relationship back together, for a whole month since Stanley's painful mistake she had been behind the scenes wielding a story of vicious lies, full of malicious intent. A neighbour had noticed Rebecca was upset, and through approaching her had discovered the reason behind Rebecca's anguish. She announced to her neighbour that she was pregnant with Stan's child, the result of a night where he had used her to help him determine his sexuality. Weaving the plot, she explained how Stan had decided he loved Rebecca and that they would raise the baby together, even get married. Then, sobbing her heart out to the poor unaware Mrs Quinn, she told her that Stan had continued his affairs with Jason. She even pretended to Mrs Quinn to be happy for them, ever playing the pitiable, deserted victim.

***

As he approached Willoughby Way, his thoughts became laced with the same guilt he had felt that day. He had been alone ever since the day when he left her and Nicole, he could never be with the woman he truly loved and for a time he thought that Nell would help ease the pain. Every day he felt more familiar with her, but it was never to be the same love that he felt for Eleanor. When he realised that this would never change, he left, after all what could he really hope for when he had introduced himself under a different name all of those years ago? In truth Henry felt that the whole relationship had been built with only one half of his personality intact, but at the time he just wanted to be someone else and start again. No longer would he have a fiancé, no longer would he have a baby daughter and he hoped that he would never have to think of Eleanor and her bewitching ways again.

Henry was wrong. When it became clear in the letters his daughter wrote that Nicole was more than just a defective child, given to the world by her mother without a care, he began to feel a tugging in his chest. They shared so much, even loved the same things and shared a momentous appreciation for architectural history. He did not know that she now worked as a personal assistant, for clothes shoppers no less! Or that she worked with the infamous Rebecca. It seemed that Nicole did not share this kind of bond with anyone else. Nell had informed him on the telephone that after he left she had broken the news to Nicole at the age of ten and she became isolated. He had called Nell in the hope that she would meet with him. Henry knew that she deserved an explanation, after all of these years she deserved more, but he could not give it to her.

Nell said that apart from a lad called Jason, Nicole had very few people around her. Henry wondered, after almost twenty years of friendship, why hadn't there been a natural progression to a relationship between Nicole and Jason? Surely Rita must have hoped. Of course it wasn't as easy as it had been in Henry's youth. You saw a pretty girl who you liked, made sure they were from a good family and then courted them until marriage. Now he felt it was all friends that occasionally sleep together or people 'seeing' each other, far too complicated he thought. He and Eleanor both knew where they stood from the very beginning. Henry's father was in the military, and being at the height of his platoon it was only natural for him to rub shoulders with land owners and higher standing socialites. Out of respect he was allowed to marry Henry's mother, the beautiful Jean Mautix and he became a Baron of Middleton.

When Henry was introduced to Eleanor she was already a Duchess, a beautiful Duchess waiting to be wed. Henry had been lucky to have her. He had competed against many other deserving gentlemen to win his prize. But Henry had not forgotten the lessons of his father and spent many hours with Eleanor's parents, clay pigeon shooting, deer hunting and participating in his favourite event, archery. He outshone all competitors from the beginning, he was confident, charming and fit. Now when Henry looked into his bathroom mirror it all felt as though it was a million miles away, almost as though it had been another lifetime. The mirror reflected an old man. His hair was graying, his skin was sagging and now his heart was giving up. It was probably no more than avid determination that kept his heart ticking over right now, and he wouldn't stop until Nicole had what was rightfully hers.

He seemed to have been holding his breath for ever. Two days had passed since he said he would meet Nell, tell her the truth. Now that time had come. He had thought and thought about how he could ask for Nell's help without telling her the truth but he knew deep down that it wouldn't work, and actually out of respect she deserved to know the truth, even if it was terrible.

He was too late. When Nell opened the door it was not happiness or gratitude that met him, but anger and frustration. She was holding something in her hand, a letter and in the other an envelope. His heart sank when he saw the handwriting. It was her writing. Shock and dismay jaded him from the irony at this point, after all of these years Eleanor had waited until now to reply to him, the only time when it was imminent that he was able to explain the delicate nature of past events to Nell, she had chosen to write now. His mind is reeling over what is in the letter, how much is he going to have to divulge, he wonders. She is standing at the door, holding it open.

Her lips are pursed, her eyes fixed on Henry, they hold a certain sadness to them. He wonders why it is that all of the women in his life end up being sad. Is it him? His own mother had died giving birth to him. There have been times when he has blamed himself for sure. He looks her in the eyes. "Can I come in please?" She steps aside without saying a word. The smell of her perfume wafts under his nose, it is slightly overbearing and he coughs a little. He notices as he edges past her that she looks particularly sultry, but she has aged badly in his absence. He can see she has attempted an effort. She wears a long fitted skirt and a purple corseted top with an oversized waterfall cardigan. The corseted top is fitted around her waist and he notices Nell's middle-aged spread. It would not be gentlemanly to stare, but Henry did notice a few deep lines across her brow and thin ones around her mouth, probably from years of chain smoking. This only reaffirms the reasons why he left her in the first place. Henry was not an aesthetic man by any means, but he knew that any woman who let herself fall in love with him was in turn allowing herself to be constantly compared to his former love. How is he going to explain?

***

I was in no rush to end this women's miserable existence. Even if the cops were looking for her, they believed she was already dead. My guess was they had given up any hope of finding her alive and had lost their sense of urgency.

It filled me with joy to see her writhe in misery as the acid ate its way through her flesh. She was sobbing hard. "If it makes you feel any better, you brought all of this on yourself," I told her as I switched on a pair of clippers. I held them to her head, wishing they were blades I could cut her open with. Maybe if I could see inside her brain I could tell why she was such a fuck up. I began shaving what was left of her hair, through partial thickness burns and blood. I stood behind her in flurry of hair, each blemished strand falling to the floor, defeated. Jason stood in front of her with a mirror. "Wow, you are ugly without your hair," he taunted. "I wonder what she'll look like without any of it?" I grinned. "How many of your 'assets' am I going to have to remove before we see the real Rebecca?" I asked, leaning in next to her ear. "What does that mean?" She said through the blubbing. "It means," I said, forcing her head back, "What were you doing pretending to be me, with my father?"

I held a pair of tweezers to her left eye. I had always been of the opinion that the left was the prettiest. Grabbing hold of four eyelashes, I began to pull, hard and slow. Gradually they tore away from her eyelid and she groaned with pain. I put them in a petri dish and placed them in her lap, she couldn't see them but she could feel them. "Please, stop!" she begged. "I really don't know what you're talking about, you must have the wrong person." To a novice this would be believable, but I knew Rebecca. I knew how sick and twisted she was. "I will find out whatever it is you're up to, even if I have to pull it out of you one piece at a time." I pulled out another four, and more and more, until there were none left and the wailing reached a formidable decibel. "Now you have nothing left on your face that you used to trick people, to steal, manipulate and hurt with. Now I want the truth."

I was impatient for answers. She looked at me with bloodshot eyes, they were pleading with me to stop, but how could I stop when I had nothing? Rebecca had just denied my every attempt to extract answers from her. I slapped her hard around the face. "Don't give me that shit, it doesn't work on me sweetheart. Now tell me, why have you been meeting with Henry?"

"She was trying... to... inherit your father's estate." The acid fumes had dried out Rebecca's throat, she kept coughing and wheezing. "What do mean, my father's estate? My father was an architect, there is no estate?" "Wollaton, it belongs to your Mother and Father." She was losing consciousness, her head lolling to the side after each word. "You were adopted, so you would not be in line to, inherit anything." I didn't believe a word of it and thought it quite amusing that Rebecca had worked so hard for nothing. Rebecca knew about Nicole's love affair with Nottingham, how she spent all her waking hours at Wollaton as a kid, Henry had obviously told her everything when he thought she was Nicki. I wondered where Henry was now, and why he had come back after all these years. "Why are you so focused on destroying her happiness? Why are you do you have to be such a bitch? Don't try to feed me some bullshit story about how you had a rough childhood! Take responsibility for yourself and your own deceit and tell me what the hell is going on!" I had a feeling my own eyes were probably bloodshot by now, with the build-up of rage in my temples.

"If I tell you will you, if I explain, will you let me go?" It was like getting puppy dog eyes from a mole. "That depends..." I paused trying to weigh her reaction, nothing. "That depends on whether or not I think you're telling me the truth and whether or not I think you deserve to be forgiven. Right now it seems you don't even care about the people you've hurt, or have any recollection for the path of destruction that lies in your past. How am I to forgive you when you look like you couldn't give a shit?" "*Please don't hurt me, it's not my fault.* It's just like her to hide away when the consequences come back to bite her, and I'm left to deal with everything." Jason pulled the rope tight around her neck, it cut into the delicate skin, now chaffed and weeping. Rebecca could barely speak. Jason pulled the rope so tight there was hardly room to breathe. I would have felt sorry for her if I hadn't known it would only take her owning up to her faults to set her free. She couldn't even manage that. Pathetic.

"How is this not your fault? You know exactly what you've done wrong, you should have to feel what others have felt when you've taken from them, used them, lied to them." All I wanted was for her to be sorry. "Please," she begged, "it's not my fault." "That's it!" I snapped, "you're not giving me anything, I can't work like this." She was angering me to the point where I was beginning not to care if she owned up to her mistakes or not, I just wanted her dead. It was as if she didn't want to realise the pain she had caused. "I can't show you the emotional pain you've caused, but I can show you physical pain," I told her, reaching for a blunt razor. Jay walked over, knowing that he was every bit as much a part of this as I was. He was here to serve his vengeance as was I. He placed each of his hands on either side of Rebecca's shaved head, and held her steady as I raised the blade to her eyebrow. I began hacking at the mousy brown hair. With each scream that emanated from Rebecca I felt justice moving closer.

After all of her facial hair was gone, Jay released her and walked away. He wasn't away long, returning with a thick woollen blanket which he wrapped around her tight. He knew this would heat her body, in turn making her sweat. The pain she would feel when the salty fluid hit her eyes would be phenomenal. Such a simple idea, yet so effective. Soon blood from the deep razor cuts slowly dribbled down over her eyelids. Rebecca blinked rapidly through her sobbing as it reached her eyes. I stepped towards her. "This seems bad now but believe me, it can get a lot worse if you don't start talking Rebecca." I was adamant I would get my answers. She gave nothing, other than tears. She just wept, trying to breathe through the stranglehold of the rope and the toxic fumes from the acid. I could tell she wanted to hang her head and cover her emotions but the rope restricted all movement. I couldn't get anything out of her. In some way she seemed to have convinced herself that none of the past events were her fault and refused to accept responsibility for any of them, referring to herself as 'she'.

Was she really going to use Nicole's condition against her? Perhaps it was Rebecca's plan to appeal to her better nature. Perhaps she thought if she could persuade Bernadette that they were the same then she would let Rebecca go. This is what she does, she gets inside your head and she twists things. Someone should put an end to it, now. Suddenly I am pulled to one side. There is a feeling in my stomach that I hadn't noticed before. I start gagging, coughing. She's rising, I can feel her. She can sense I have gone too far, she can't bear to see another human in pain. Deep breaths seem to help but how to still the churning in my stomach? She can't be here, not now. She can't be a part of this.

***

He stands in the kitchen holding his trilby. She doesn't offer to take his coat or invite him to sit at the table. Henry looks around the place. The walls in the living room now bear a yellowy tinge not unlike Nell's teeth, and he can see that she hasn't decorated since he left. The kitchen was still painted a bright yellow, tiled with white and yellow flower patterns. The units are all cheap wood and the floor is reminiscent of the eighties with its grey lino. He notices around five empty vodka bottles queuing at the back door, surrounded by a few empties of wine and beer containers. She catches his eye. "I haven't had a drink in weeks now." she scowls. "Oh." Henry choked, hoping he hadn't stepped on a land mine. "Did it have you in its clutches huh? It's easy to get carried away sometimes isn't it?" He was trying to break the ice, but Nell wasn't having any of it. "It was a bit more than that, I've pretty much been in a coma since you left, sorry what do I call you?" She didn't waste any time getting to the crux of the matter.

"Perhaps you should sit down." Henry gestured to the chair at the kitchen table.

"Don't you dare tell me what to do!" she spat, her cheeks now reddening, evident of years of alcohol abuse. "Ok" he said, "but I am going to sit." He pulls out the chair, sits down. "I've been talking with Nicole, she met me at the train station." He's not sure how much Nell knows, but can detect that already he's said something to worsen the situation. "So how should I address you then, *Henry*?" "Yes, my name is Henry and I am a coward." he pleaded, genuinely sorry for everything. "So you still love her then? That's why you left, but if you still love her why aren't you with her?" Nell seemed to be calming now, as though it was only the truth she wanted, not some begging apology and a promise to make it all up to her. After all it had been eighteen years now, what could she really expect? "I will always love Eleanor, but she is not without her troubles, that is the reason I left."

Nell is still holding the letter in her hand. "Can I see?" he asks, even though the letter is addressed to him. She unfolds her arms and hands him the letter. Now he will know the extent of information that Nell knows. "Why didn't you tell me she was yours?" she says with frustration in her voice. "You know I would have raised another woman's baby the same no matter where it had come from." Henry is saddened because he knows it is true. Nell wasn't just desperate for a baby for herself, but she had wanted to bear a child for him so that they could be a family. "Yes, I do know that. You have to understand, I mean I was in a terrible place then. We had only been together for nine months, everything had moved so quickly, we were living together, we were getting married and then the baby arrived. I just didn't know what else to do." Her eyes reflect the disappointment she felt when Henry had not been as happy as she had been back then. He must have been pretending to her the whole time, it had all been a lie. "How was she, after not seeing you in so many years?" Nell felt her own guilt now. When Henry left, Nell had drowned herself in booze, it was not just him that had missed out on Nicole growing up. In fact she had probably communicated more to Henry through their letters over the years than any mutterings and groans that she and Nell had exchanged. "It wasn't her, I know that now, but I didn't realise until it was too late. She knows everything." Henry could add this to the list of everything else that he felt guilty about. A complete stranger who somehow knew who Henry was, had met him at the train station pretending to be his daughter. Had she gotten away with it, he suspected there would have been the exchange of money in her favour.

Even when Henry realised her true intentions, he realised she would have then continued to bribe him in return for her silence. This, among other reasons, was why he had not confronted the little blood sucker. Nell piped up, "Was it the same woman you were with in the paper?" Henry's face is now a deep purple red, he looks as though he is holding his breath. The veins and capillaries in his cheeks look as though they might burst. "Henry?" she enquires as he falls to the floor, clutching his chest and coughing. The wooden chair caused a racket as it flew out from underneath his slim build, into the wood effect cupboard panels. He lay there braced, thinking this may be it. The Doctor had warned him that should he postpone surgery, he would be treading on risky ground. He thought he was fitter, too fit to have a heart attack, and he was. Henry had been a builder and an architect all his life, he was not adverse to physical labour. He ate a Mediterranean diet and took a daily dose of multi vitamins. The condition that had Henry Middleton lying on the floor gasping for air would stay with him as long as he lived. To be rid of it would require him to travel into the past and not meet her, it would take missing out on seeing his beautiful queen, she is what he thought of now. Henry Middleton was dying of a broken heart.

She could hear the ambulance wailing, it sounded as though it was about a mile away still. Nell was knelt beside him as he lay ceased on her kitchen floor. She had thought about seeing him in pain for many years now, she longed for him to suffer as she had. But now, seeing him on the brink of death, she felt only love. He squeezed her hand tight and thought of Eleanor. Was he too late to ever see her again? Should he die in hospital, they would never let her out to see him. He wouldn't want her to see him this way. He wanted her to see him as the man when they first met before, him. He knew that Eleanor had been paying him, for the baby and to stay out of the press, and she had begged Henry never to find him. It had taken all the strength he could muster to not pay him a visit he'd never forget; but they had to think of their reputation. Eleanor was clearly sick by then and it wouldn't have taken much for the press to get their filthy hands on two front page stories. All he ever wanted to do was protect her, that's why he had to let them take her. He wasn't sure if he belonged in there too, he had been but a shell of a man since it happened. Now his shell was giving up on him, perhaps it was for the best. Henry had never been much of a religious man, though he respected the depictions of cherubim and angels in all the places he had worked, he had never felt that personal attachment to God or any other deity. Suddenly his chest had become loose. He could breathe again. His whole body relaxed and wave after wave of tranquillity passed over him. He did not hear the ambulance arrive as it screeched around the corner, the sound of cascading wheelie bins toppling off the pavement as it did so.

"Hello, Mrs Singer? Are you the one who called the ambulance?" Nell looked up, startled. "Yes, yes! Please, hurry. I think he's going unconscious," she panicked. The paramedics walked over to Henry. The look on the male paramedic's face told Nell it wasn't good news. "What's his name love?" The paramedic asked Nell, while the woman fitted a breathing mask onto Henry's ashen face. She couldn't draw away from looking at Henry, she still had so many questions to ask him. "Henry," she eventually mumbled after having to think for a second. As she breathed out his name she thought about what it meant, Henry. She never really had him, did she? He had given her a false name and a false life to match. She had even taken his name in anticipation that they would be married soon, and so that Nicole would not be teased at school for having unwed parents.

What about Nicole? The poor girl won't know what to believe, she thought. After years of wondering who her real parents are, this is what she gets. She couldn't think about that any more. It was what had driven her to drink in the first place. Nicole had been such an independent young girl, taking after her father, exploring the city. After Nell told her she was adopted she hadn't seen Nicole for days. Rita had been kind enough to leave a message that she was with her, staying on Jason's bedroom floor. She had just about been coherent enough to register the information coming through the answering machine as she lay slumped on the sofa, barely clinging onto a near empty litre bottle of vodka. She remembers feeling proud that it had lasted her to the end of the day. Henry was not the only one who had let her down. She hoped with all her heart that he would live and that both of them could work together to save Nicole's broken past. Her thoughts were drawn back to the present as the legs of the stretcher snapped into place, and the paramedics began wheeling Henry through the hallway. She grabbed her coat and closed the door as they headed into the ambulance. All three of their futures were in the hands of the surgeons now, Nell prayed that they could perform a miracle.

Chapter Fifteen: Pushing The Envelope

Maybe if I left her alone to think on things for a while I would stand more of a chance. Perhaps then she would tell me something. Time to reflect could be the key. "Jay and I are leaving now. You are staying here, alone. It will give you time to think of a reason why we shouldn't kill you. Think about it Rebecca, can you honestly say you deserve to live?" I asked, trying to get her to look at me. She was a wreck and I had only just started, I had nothing to show for it. Jay checked her hands, neck and feet while she sobbed. The rope was already tight but he made sure she wasn't going anywhere by tightening it further. She looked petrified and completely humiliated. I knew Nicole would never have been able to reach this stage. I was happy to do it for her, that's what I did. Jay moved next to me and together we headed for the door. I switched off the light and we walked through the large corrugated door, slamming it shut behind us. We lingered at the other side of the door before moving away. We swapped glances as we both heard Rebecca weeping in the darkness. For the first time there was nobody to save her, no-one to manipulate into helping her, no-one to feel sorry for her and clean up her mess. For the first time Rebecca Singer was alone.

Outside, Jay poured himself a cup of herbal from his thermos flask. It had been a hell of a long week and we had both missed a lot of sleep. The adrenalin and police parties hadn't helped but now I crawled into the van and wrapped a blanket around my body. I felt frail but there was no turning back, not now. I lay my head down on my rucksack and within minutes I am drifting.

Jason finishes his tea. He is about to join Bernadette to rest when he hears something. It is coming from the warehouse. He edges closer but can't see through the closed door. It sounds like laughing but it's broken and unfamiliar. After a minute of trying to decipher the noise, tiredness gets the better of him and he climbs in the van next to Bernie. He looks at her for a few seconds, wondering who he may wake up next to in the morning.

She woke up to the sound of Jason brushing his teeth. He was using a bottle of spring water to rinse his toothbrush. She opened the van door, called out to him. "Why don't you just use the river? It's only quarter of a mile away." He shrugs, knowing that it is because if he finds himself walking away he might not come back. They spend half an hour freshening up from a long overdue night's sleep and recalibrate. It was time to start all over again. Bernadette stood before the door, thinking about what they were doing.

Nicole needed to carry out the things she wasn't capable of. Things she dreamt of but could never even contemplate doing. I would help rid her of her pain; after all, whatever she felt, I had to deal with too, and Rebecca Pierce was one problem I wasn't willing to put up with anymore. I looked at

Jason, finishing his tea. "Ready?" I asked. "Ready." he replied.

The door burst open, lights came on bright making my eyes sting, that along with sweat. It had crept down the rough surface of my head and into my naked eyes. I was in agony, struggling to breathe. The rope around my neck, so tight. My hands had been tied together so tightly that they were numb. That bitch. Who did she think she was? Questioning me, questioning my behaviour. Not once had I ever felt the need or compulsion to explain myself. I acted with careful thought, planning, I committed to my deceit. What had she ever done? Except chastise me for achieving my goals. Jealousy won't get you anywhere, I thought as I sneered at the open doorway.

She didn't even flinch. "Rebecca!" I shouted in her face. Then from nowhere came an awful smile, the feeling of dread in my stomach confirmed. Her head tilted to the side as though she were trying to understand who I was. "Rebecca you say...." she asked in a questioning manner as though she were confused by the name. "Yes I know her, pretty little thing. Such beautiful hair... long hair." For a reason only known to Rebecca, she had started speaking in the ways of an old hag witch. She was beginning to resemble something from a bad adaption of a Shakespeare play. I had to seriously consider the possibility that Rebecca was mentally unstable. I gave it one more shot. "Let me make this clear. Right now and for the foreseeable future I hold the key to your life. If you fail to give me what I want, you will suffer." I spoke to her as I would a child. The response was minimal, she continued to stare blankly.

I enjoyed agitating her, this bitch had it in for Rebecca from the start. All I'd ever tried to do was make life easier for her, get her what she wanted. "Rebecca is a better person than you'll ever be Bernadette."

I had turned my back on her in an attempt to gather my options if Rebecca continued to be awkward. I swung around sharply on hearing her response. "What do you mean? Are you suggesting that you've taken was owed to you, is that how you justify it?" I failed to hide my confusion, and frustration that I literally didn't know who I was speaking to. At the same time as trying to understand the meaning of her words, I was also processing the fact that Rebecca seemed to be referring to herself as a different person. Either way, she was just furthering my opinion that she was a selfish bitch, out for number one only. I decided to stick to the point, the gut feeling that brought me here in the first place, that and Jason.

I wasn't the only one who was confused. Jay lingered in the background, out of Rebecca's sight behind her, wearing a frown. His arms were folded across his chest, clearly stating he was agitated. Whatever he felt, it seemed he didn't feel able to convey it to the person in front of him. Again Rebecca just stared as if it was only *her* words that mattered. "Don't you feel anything for the people whose lives you've ruined? Tell me why you think it's ok to sabotage the lives of others for you own gain." It was like talking at a brick wall.

They ran towards her forehead rapidly as if they were aiming for the already painful eye area. Her underarms were sodden with perspiration, although she had somehow managed to shrug away the thick woollen blanket supplied by Jason. This angered me as it alluded to the fact that Rebecca probably thought she would be able to wriggle free. She was undermining me and it just added to my purpose.

I took a step forward and lowered my lips to her bloodied ear. "You've had time to consider your options. Will you help or hinder? If you give me the answers I'm looking for you will be helping yourself." I took a step back in preparation for her reply. Slowly she began to raise her head, her eyes holding contact with the floor all the while. They lifted gradually, starting at my feet and making their way up my body until they made contact with my own suspecting eyes. Taken aback, I had to hide my alarm as the sight of Rebecca's face staggered me somewhat. Jason had loosened the rope but her neck was still etched with red lines and deep cuts. Streaks of blood and sweat stained her flushed face, and each eye was a map of red rivers holding anger and rage. I backed away, not knowing what to do with the shock I was feeling. She looked as though she was about to say something, perhaps reveal to me the answers I needed. To begin with this had been nothing more than a personal lesson to Rebecca. A warning so that she may change her ways. Now it had become personal, now Rebecca had interfered with my family and I wanted to know why. I waited for her to speak.

She tried to find remorse in me but I had none. Rebecca wouldn't be where she was today without me. "Do you think it's easy getting what you want? Befriending these idiots until they trust me, until I have them in a vice? Do you think I like listening to them whine about their miserable lives, their dirty little secrets? Do you think I even want to acknowledge these people?" She corrected herself, "these losers? Who wouldn't exploit morons like them, I'd have to be a fool myself and I am no fool."

I stepped back, almost physically thrown by the strength and intensity of her words. I didn't know why I hadn't expected it and I silently cursed myself for being temporarily naive. "Ok, so they're idiots, right?" I asked because I really did want to understand Rebecca's odd sense of reasoning, the type of reasoning that only a deluded mad woman would hold value to.

"Yes, they deserved everything they got." She answered with such a self assured smile. and nodded the words at me as though I might have been inclined to agree with the crazy bitch.

"You don't think you have any duty towards them after what you did?" I questioned.

"So I ripped a few people off, stole a couple of jobs, nailed some woman's husband... or three..." She trailed off giggling to herself, obviously tickled by her own admission. "What's the big deal? No-one's dead!" She gave me a look that told me I was over-reacting, the sort of look that made me want to slap her back to another dimension. How could she not get it? The only aspect of what she had done, that made what she had done ok, was that nobody had been killed. Nobody had been killed, therefore no-one had suffered. In Rebecca's mind, that was the truth. Although I may have been coming around to understanding Rebecca's sick sense of reasoning, I wasn't about to let her think that it was acceptable. I hadn't come this far to make her a martyr. No, she would have to pay the price, one way or another. "Rebecca, what if these things were done to you?" I asked, hoping for a truthful insight, hoping that perhaps she had never viewed it from their side of the fence before and that she may shoulder some guilt.

"If someone hoodwinked me as well as I have, I'd say fair play. Only complete degenerates lose out, and believe me, they are. Luckily I'm not stupid enough to leave myself open to..."

Slap, slap, slap. The sound of the front and back of my hand hitting Rebecca's face hard snapped through the air like cracking ice. Jason jumped out of his head and was paying attention, his eyes wide open.

"Apologise for what you've done!" I yelled in her face, I had run out of patience, if I ever had any to start with.

"No."

"Tell me why you do these terrible things!"

"Because I love to desecrate everything close to the heart. Come on Bernie, look inside, are you truly happy?" She asked with her head tilted to the side like a dog begging for a treat.

"Not right now because I'm talking to a mad woman who thinks the world is hers for the taking and doesn't give a shit about anything or anyone in it. Say you're sorry!" I screamed, shaking her by the shoulders.

"NO!"

"Just admit it, admit you're wrong!"

"NO!"

I couldn't take anymore, my heart pounding in my chest, threatening to burst through my rib cage. I let my hands slide off her and turned to walk away.

"Oh don't stop now Bernie, you're starting to turn me on. Thought we were getting somewhere, you know developing a bond." I pursed my lips together not knowing where to go next, what to do with her body after I'd drained the life from it. The same image began replaying in my head; me with my hands squeezing around Rebecca's throat, until every last wicked breath had left her body. But that would be too kind for a woman who held nothing dear, no-one close and didn't even see anything wrong with it. All she had ever done was betray people, hurt people, tear their lives apart until there was nothing left. I didn't see remorse when I looked at her, and I really had looked, striving to find a singular fleck of regret in her twisted psyche, but anything I could find was self-satisfying. She was an empty vessel fuelled by anger and loathing. Nell always said I should pick my battles wisely. I had chosen badly and I feared I was about to lose. Taking a deep breath, I knew I couldn't let Rebecca read my thoughts, I had to see this through.

Not wanting to show any weakness, I strolled gracefully (as not to rush) over to Jason. He had the tip of his thumb between his teeth, contemplating what had just taken place. He put his arm around me and dropped his head. "Don't worry B, I don't expect you to get an apology out of her for me. She's obviously a lunatic." He looked resigned. "I don't think we should give up Jay, I mean what about all those other people?" I asked, unsure of whether my enthusiasm could last much longer. "They didn't know who screwed them over then, they're not going to know now, let's just leave it?" The thought of just letting Rebecca go made my head pound. It wasn't an option, pure and simple.

After a few more minutes, with Rebecca chatting to herself about how rude it is to turn your back on someone, mumbling obscenities about private conversations when you have company and a condensed lengthy discussion, Jay and I came to a decision. Rebecca's fate was in our hands, the last and only payback we would ever have.

I ambled back to my spot in front of the contained Rebecca and absorbed the smart arsed look in her face. *Not for long* I thought, *not for long*. Jay gave me a knowing look as his eyes found mine over the top of Rebecca's head, away from her gaze.

"What are you smirking at?!" Rebecca's voice snapped the vibes between Jay and I, breaking it and tossing it aside as if it were meaningless. It was almost as though she knew. "Sorry Rebecca, we know you're not used to being sidelined, didn't mean to disregard your presence." She could sense my sarcasm and it achieved the desired effect. Spit flailed from her lips as she spat vilely towards me. "How dare you disrespect me! I will not be, nor have I ever been ignored! You should be giving my ring the royal licking you piece of shit. You don't know anything about what it is to survive. Mummy and daddy gave you everything, probably still wiping your arse for you, you little prick! Don't ever walk away from me again. You *will* give me the respect I am owed, lest you learn a lesson the hard way. To start you can begin calling me by *my* name, hers is pathetic, weak." Her chin fell inward to rest on her chest. It was as though the massive outburst had used up all of her energy and now she sat there looking at the floor, chest heaving as it expelled air out of her lungs. Apart from her heavy sighs, she was completely silent, as if nothing had happened. She resembled a robot which had run out of fuel, lifeless.

We were floored. Neither I nor Jay knew whether to laugh or grimace. The fact that Rebecca seemed to think everything was owed to her was beyond me. I couldn't understand how anyone could think that way. I couldn't understand why if Rebecca saw something she wanted, she would take it regardless of whether she should or not, whether it was right or wrong. Studying Rebecca while my thoughts lingered in a trance, I noticed how her bottom lip was sticking out slightly. Rebecca was sulking! Her behaviour was like that of a child who had failed to get their own way. If her arms had been free, perhaps they would now be folded across her chest in protest, and her feet stomping on the stone floor. My thoughts jumped into action as I remembered the last thing Rebecca said. *'Call me by my name.'*

Chapter Sixteen: Grey Area

What did she mean? I could only think of several names for her, but none that she would like. Humouring her, I asked. "So what's this new name you've given yourself?" Rebecca had taken on the attitude of a stroppy teenager. I was almost certain she would begin pulling faces when I wasn't looking in her direction. But then her eyes took on a noticeable blackness that I hadn't seen before, and I felt bile rise in my stomach. She was conjuring something, I could feel it. It was like the air around her changed. Similar to how the air changes on a hot sunny day just before a storm. I started to brace myself. Even Jason took a step back and all he could see was the back of her head.

Her mouth smiled a tight line across her face, showing a wickedness that made me shiver. Slowly raising her dark eyes, sneering, she told me, "The name's Susie, I'll tell you everything you want to know." Then her face stretched into a frowning grin, only reaping joy from the misery of others. Susie? Who was Susie? Was this another one of her tricks, a way of worming out of yet another sticky situation? I had no choice but to go along with it, test the water.

"Ok Susie, perhaps you can shed some light on Rebecca's life, why *is* she such a bitch?"

"You can't do that."

"Do what?"

"You're about to give Rebecca all the credit for *my* hard work. That won't do."

"What do you mean? Tell me how you've got anything to do with this." Aside from just being a distraction for Jay and I while Rebecca works on an escape route, I thought.

"I can tell you how I fucked Jay's boyfriend, how I made up the pregnancy to split them up. I have nothing to blame my behaviour on, I get what I want and I don't see anything wrong with that. I do have a problem with everyone giving Rebecca credit for something *I* have done all by myself." She let out a deep rippling laugh, amused by her own admission. Where was the guilt? There were no signs of remorse. I couldn't get my head around it. Perhaps I was dealing with a mad woman. If that was the case, how would I go about understanding the actions of someone who was seemingly unstable? How could I decide what was forgivable or unforgivable, moral or amoral? I couldn't deceiver whether blame would still lie with Rebecca if I discovered that she wasn't exactly wholly responsible for everything she had done. I had to rethink our plan. Kneeling down in front of Rebecca I felt the same thing I had been feeling since I first crossed her. Defeat. Somehow the tables had turned once again and she was forcing me to doubt myself when I was so sure I was doing the right thing.

"It's like looking in the mirror isn't it?" she whispered, leaning forward slightly. I looked into her eyes, I was searching for something, lots of things. Remorse, the truth. I was looking for anything that may help give clues to how I should deal with

Rebecca. She didn't try to stop me, there were no signs of her feeling uncomfortable. For the first time I began to feel as though we were equal, level somehow. Perhaps we were more similar than I thought. As much as it sickened me, there was a chance that Rebecca shared my condition. My heart skipped a beat as I realized I had overstepped the line. As a last resort to find out the truth, I asked her, "Did Rebecca have *any* say in what you did?" She inhaled deeply and I realized I was holding my breath.

"She doesn't know anything, she just thinks everything kept turning out peachy 'cos she's such a nice person." Although I had to accept that Rebecca wasn't responsible for her actions, I still couldn't neglect the feelings of anger I had towards Rebecca's alter ego. I rose to my feet and took a few steps away from her, as if by watching her from a distance would enable me to see further in to the situation. She was still smiling impiously. "I can do anything I want. I can make a man beg to have me, or a woman if that's what I feel like. Bet I could even have Jay giving me head if you left us alone for five minutes." Her laugh became low and grizzly, almost as though she were possessed. She was so crude. I couldn't believe I had blamed everything on Rebecca. I had to act. "Jay, gag her." I had reformed the plan, I couldn't hurt Rebecca anymore. Jay rushed towards her with the elongated bandana. "Fuck you gay boy. You know Stan hated you, he begged me to get him away from you, you and your expectations. He was just too weak to tell you he was bored!"

She began laughing uncontrollably, rocking back and forth. Gathering momentum, she began biting at Jay's hands as he tried to force the material between her dry pale lips. She growled at Jason, her eyes loaded with fury. Jason chose his moment carefully but just before he could shove the material in she spat, "Your Mother is retarded." Jason looked at me, wondering who it was she was directing the insult to. "I'm talking to you sweet cheeks," she seethed, pulling her head away from the gag. "She lives in old mental block at Rampton." Another poisonous laugh before Jason finally shoved the material into her mouth, stretching the corners of her parched lips into a twisted smile. She struggled as he secured it with a tight knot at the back of her shaven head. Belligerent eyes followed me as I gathered speed towards Rebecca.

Grabbing her around the chin, I explained, "I will not listen to you anymore. You are without a doubt the most vile specimen of evil I have ever had the misfortune of meeting. I hope for Rebecca's sake that you seek forgiveness for your crimes against humanity, because until you do, you're both going to a place where neither of you can be hurt and your freedom will be limited as way of punishment. It's time to make a decision; only one of you can survive." The blade had been there for several minutes now, before Rebecca said softly, "I know who your father is," her eyes trying to reach Bernadette's behind her. "I know who my father is!" Bernadette hissed through her teeth. Rebecca sighed. "I know who your real father is." Bullshit. Even if there was any truth to what she was saying, Bernadette refused to give in, to give her the satisfaction or the power by asking her to elaborate. She pressed the knife in until the skin on her jugular flushed red.

She had thought that if she offered Nicole some information then they might let her go, but it seemed only to anger her more. "I have no control over her you know, I don't have a say in anything, she just does what she wants and I'm left to pick up the pieces." Rebecca is weeping gently now as to not aggravate the blade where it being held steadily. Bernadette knows this is all sounding a little too familiar. She knows when she is in charge there is only one thing that can put Nicki back on top again, Jason. What if Rebecca is telling the truth, what if she doesn't have an anchor and... What if she's been torturing the wrong person all along? No, it was too easy. Rebecca obviously knew, somehow about Nicole and she was using it to get to her and wriggle out of yet another compromising situation. The reality of the steel blade slicing her open moved closer with each lie she spoke.

"Bernie I think we should stop," Jason pleaded.

"It's lies, it's all lies, why won't she just stop lying?" She didn't know if it was purely the idea that Rebecca claimed to know more about Nicole's past than she did but she refused to believe it. "She'll say anything to get out of being accountable Jason, don't listen to her!" She was staring hard at the broken body in front of her. She was holding a kitchen knife to her throat, all the while trying to fight Nicole, she was getting stronger. "Jason, you have to calm down, if you don't I won't be able to hold her down, she's drawn to you." Jason knew that Nicki had always been there for him as he had for her. They had spent so much time together growing up and he had kept her secret, he wondered now if he should have told her. "What if she's telling the truth Bernie?" He would not give up on her, not yet. "Look at what you're doing, right now you're no better than she is." Maybe he would get through to her this way. "I've had enough Jason, I'm going to finish her." She was looking at him as though she wanted him to stop her but then something flashed over her eyes and she was gone again, now she whispers in Rebecca's ear, "Is that what you want, Susie or whatever your name is? If I slit your throat no-one will even miss you." Rebecca lets out a ripple of laughter as the blade scratches the already wounded skin on her throat.

It was clear to Jason that this had become about more than just revenge. Bernadette was fast heading down a road he dare not venture. If Doctor Hammond or the police found out how far this had gone, Nicki would never see the light of day again. He had to do something. "I'm leaving Bernie. If you don't stop then you're in this on your own, it's gone too far, I want out." Her eyes were now focused on Jason. "You want out?" She sneered at Jason. "Do you think I want to be doing this? I'm only doing it for her!" Her words boomed around the room, bouncing back to the middle. "I think you believed you were doing it for her but now..." He looked to the floor. The cold concrete was beginning to form ice puddles, winter was setting in. "Go on Jason, say what you really think!" She snapped, pointing the blade in his direction. He was standing by the door ready to run, he had already unbolted the hinges ready for a swift escape, should he need it.

"When was the last time I saw Nicole? It seems like you're here all the time, I miss her." He was trying to reason with her, but it was only fuelling the fire. It was true that he was Nicole's friend first, Bernie was an extra that he vowed to endure for Nicki's sake. She had been there for him through the rough school years, and her kind heart had lent itself to him before any of her own troubles. "You miss her, that wimp? Am I not good enough for you, is that it?" She was scowling hard, taking steps towards him now, aiming the knife at his chest. Susie is chuckling in the background, her head now lulling forwards, bobbing up and down as she mocks them. "I'm trying to help you you stupid cow, shut up!" Jason yells over the top of Bernadette's shoulder. He looks to the knife at the centre of his chest, fear now taking over his face as he now looks to saving his own life. "I know you were only ever trying to protect her Bernie, but I think..."

The knife makes a clattering sound as it drops to the floor. "Trying to protect who? Who are you talking to?" Fear and panic gather into one as she looks around the room. "Jason, where are we, who is that, why is she bleeding, have we been kidnapped?" Then silence fills the room as Nicole collapses to the floor. He kneels beside her and checks her pulse. Susie is laughing hysterically, choking and coughing, her lips cracked and parched from the fumes. He didn't know if it was the shock of her surroundings and the constant pressure of Bernadette's presence that had made her pass out, or if Bernie had inhaled the same fumes that now had Rebecca in a semi conscious state, either way he knew what he had to do. For years he had coped with the two friends he had lying in front of him now, for years he had managed to balance a friendship with them both, knowing that the end goal was the same for them both, to protect Nicole. Now he was out of his depth, he knew Nicole wouldn't want this and felt awful that his request upon Bernie to help him was now putting Nicole's future at risk. He steps outside, taking in the fresh winter air, it had actually been colder inside the warehouse. He waited anxiously as the dial tone rang, the receiver picked up. "Mum? I need you."

He had to work fast, now more than ever. Not only because he had skipped the surgery, discharging himself from hospital early in order to find Nicole, but to tell her, to explain everything, he owed her that much. He had to see her before it was too late, for him and Nicole. Rita had phoned Nell asking for the hospital's number, she'd had to lie, telling them she was a relative. What she had to tell Henry had to be heard directly as to not involve the police. Jason had only told her the bare minimum, that it was a lesson gone bad and that they needed help. Rita was parked outside the Trinity when he exited, still ripping off band aids and the ends of clear tubing they had attached when he was unconscious. His heart pounded as he opened the door to Rita's Saab. Rita had aged well, she was a good Catholic woman who had been at their wedding. Henry had confided in her the day he had Eleanor institutionalized. Rita had told him that one day the Devil would release Eleanor from his wicked grasp and she would be given to him again. He was still waiting for that day, but for now, it was all that he could do to save his daughter.

She knew it was the world she was doing a favour, not just Nicole. Without Rebecca around, the world would be better off. Nicki was growing stronger somehow, but she had made sure it wouldn't happen again, she had locked herself in, out of Jason's reach. The chemicals fizzed and sizzled as they twisted around each other, reacting and hissing, fumes billowing above the bucket. This way was better. This way it would be slow, painful. It would be everything she deserved.

The drive from town had taken about an hour. They had driven through the night and now the early dawn rose in front of them. It should have taken longer, but where Jason was concerned, Rita's safety came second. The car had ducked and weaved through traffic, all while with Rita trying to see out of a little hole she had made in the ice on the windscreen. Normally Henry would be petrified, but he was saving his heart for Nicole, he had to last the journey even if his was to end soon. Soon they were met by the Forest. Henry knew that although it was a part of the New Forest, very few people knew about it. Nicole had done her research well, he had to proud of her for that. Rita had explained in the car that Jason and Nicki had both been spited by the same woman, that she was out to ruin them at every turn.

Henry remembered seeing the story in the paper about Rebecca Pierce's house burning down, and also the trajectory rumours that stemmed from it concerning her and the major. He often read the Nottingham weekly online at home, just to make sure mostly. If this was the same woman that had come to him in the guise of Nicki, then he leaned toward understanding why they may have gone to such lengths to assault her. He wondered what she had done to Nicole and what she had told her so far. They abandoned the car in a small clearing just inside the woods. To anyone who was looking the car would be visible through the undergrowth but to the untrained eye it was easily camouflaged. The forest floor was hard in places, scattered twigs that would normally snap under foot just squished into the mud, soggy and defrosted after the ice.

She had managed to kick the bucket away after holding her breath for just over a minute. She knew that Nicole had been affected by the fumes from the acid earlier, now that she had mixed it with acid, the same chemical process was happening inside her body. The match had left her fingers just before she had passed out; the explosion had sent Rebecca careering to the floor, blowing her chair over. The warehouse now burned fiercely, the glass in the top windows smashing from the rising heat. She could hear the door being rattled, it was Jason, they had been locked in. Susie knew where she had put the key but she wasn't telling. Toxic fumes were gathering above them now, if she didn't find the key soon they would both be dead. She snakes on her stomach to Nicole's limp body and begins patting down her silhouette, feeling for any lumps or jagged edges. She cannot see what she is looking for, with the gas and smoke burning her eyes and blocking her vision. Eventually her hand gets stuck on something. She hurriedly reaches inside Nicole's pocket and grasps the keys.

There are three padlocks above her head, she steadies herself against the cold iron circle. She is thankful that it is still cold. A fallen shard of glass pierces the skin on her hand as she scrambles to climb up the door. She has reached the first lock and inserted the key. Blood begins to trickle down her inner thighs, it had mixed with the acid and it burns on the delicate skin. She winces as she reaches the second lock, it pops open and she drops both of the padlocks to the floor. Her head is spinning viciously, she cannot focus on the top lock. The sweat is dripping from her forehead, the lack of eyebrows and eyelashes allowing it to cascade into her burning retinas. She fumbles with the top lock once more, but she is beginning to lose consciousness, and her legs crumble from underneath her. She tumbles and lands face first on the floor, her blood pumping furiously to her vital organs, trying to keep her alive. For a moment, for a split second she is worried, then everything fades to white.

After fifty paces they could smell the smoke. Henry knew instantly it was no ordinary fire, he picked up the toxic gas instantly as it evaporated into the atmosphere. They came to a wide trunk; Jason had left instructions to go straight ahead when they got to the largest trunk. He hadn't specified that it was an Oak, but it was the only one surrounded by younger thinner trees. They pressed on ahead of the tree, Rita stopping to tie a red ribbon around one of its branches. The wind was blowing south in their direction and the fumes were becoming stronger. Henry worried that soon they would have company if anyone reported seeing smoke in the forest. The local authorities had never taken too kindly to people picnicking and hiking in non designated areas. Usually because it was a drain on their resources, having to send a team of men out to find a family who were lost because Dad lost the compass. People often underestimated the power of the forest and its effect on disorientating a person's perception of their geographical surroundings. The smoke filled his nostrils now; they had walked another fifty paces and stopped to see billows of smoke rising from the derelict warehouse.

His heart struggled with the walk and the knowledge that he might not be able to save his daughter. Something must have gone terribly wrong, why would they set fire to the building? Henry hoped with all his being that it wasn't Nicole who had started the fire, he hoped that she steered clear completely of her Mother's way of thinking. First they saw the large transit van perched outside, they must have come into the forest from the other side. The sounds of Mickey's banging were drowned out by the urgency surrounding the fire, only Jason and Nicole knew he was there.

They hurried to the door to find Jason banging and barging the door, he was not getting anywhere. "she's locked it from the inside" he says breathlessly to Henry. He looks to Rita. "Mum!" For the first time in four days, he feels he can pass the reins over, share the burden. "Lord help ya soon, what ya got ya self into now?" He looks at the floor then steps towards Rita, throwing his arms around her. "I'm so sorry Mum, it was all my idea. I think she may have killed her." Henry could tell that part of the door was loose; it was just the very top lock that seemed to be holding the door shut. Rita's husband had left a crowbar in the boot which she passed to Henry. Instantly he began tearing away iron panels from the right side of the door, his heart aching with each effort. Eventually he had made a hole big enough for one person to clamber through. Rita and Jason agreed to stay outside while Henry crawled in.

First he came to Rebecca, the woman who would have swindled him if he had believed she was his daughter. He would not have recognised her had Jason not told him she had been there. He grimaced as he realised this was the work of his own daughter, what was she thinking? The poor girl had no eyelashes, her eyebrows had been hacked away. There were more than six deep cuts on her scalp from which she was bleeding badly. They were both unconscious, though he could just about see through the fog of smoke that Rebecca had managed to put Nicole in the recovery position and thrown a blanket over her head. Rebecca lay bleeding, there was no barrier between her and the toxic clouds. He crawled on his belly towards Nicole, he rolled her into his arms and saw Eleanor. He was struck by how she had inherited all of Eleanor's beauty, but Eleanor had been plagued with a darkness of the mind and he wondered if his beautiful Nicole had suffered the same condition. Looking at Rebecca he knew, but he did not want to admit that she was her Mother's daughter. He crouched down by the square hole in the wall, feeling relief and breathing in the cooler air. He passed her legs through to Jason, making sure she didn't catch on the sharp edges of the panel.

Someone approached from the side of the building, scattering leaves underfoot. Doctor Hammond sprinted the last twenty metres. "You found them?" he asked Rita. "We've been looking for these two for days," he said, looking at Jason's guilty face and Nicole's limp body on the bed of leaves. "Jason called when it got too much Doctor, he's not a bad boy really, I swear." Rita wanted to protect Jason. It had not been easy for him growing up and she knew she had taught him well, but Rita would always forgive before scorning. "You did the right thing calling me Jason." the Doctor kneeled over Nicole, while Henry clambered back through the hole into the furnace to search for Rebecca. Rita looked at Jason. "Do you think she'll ever forgive ya boy?" "I'm not sure Mum, but at least she might live to hate me now." He didn't know how, but he managed the beginnings of a smile. Although he was worried for Nicole, part of him had begun to relax, knowing that the adults were here and that they were going to make everything ok, at least that's what he hoped. Henry got inside and realised her body was missing.

None of them had noticed the door creep open, even with the roaring flames sounding in the background. She had found the knife. They had completely humiliated her, ruined her plans and taken away everything she needed to live happily. There would be no more free cinema tickets, no more three dates a week, paid for. Who wants to date a girl with hair that grows in tufts? The damage from the acid didn't hurt but it made her angry. The skin had melted away and all that was left was raw muscle and fat, it would take some serious surgery to repair. But Rebecca doesn't plan on going anywhere near a hospital, she knows she may never be allowed back out.

Chapter Seventeen: History Repeated

Her bed is tidy and neat. It is one of the only tasks she performs in here that reminds her of her former life. The paintings on the walls add colour now and she is surrounded by their faces, but she is still alone.

It had been nearly a week since she had sent the letter, now she waited alone in her room for his return. In her mind they were father and daughter living happily, awaiting her return so that they may be a family for the very first time. It had been a long twenty eight years and she longed to gaze upon them both and hold them close to her. But she knew in the deepest parts of her soul that it was nothing more than a dream. Once there had been hope, a bright light now dimmed and blackened by dark clouds of doubt. It was the same doubt that had torn them apart, the same blackness that had swallowed her future. It had been her only lifeline, after years of solitude hope was her only friend. Now it faded into the past along with everything else. They did not suspect her, good behaviour over the long period she had spent here had earned her an easel, paintbrushes and paints. She had painted them many times. Mac had been to see her over thirteen years ago, he came for money, all he ever came for was money. She had given it to him, accepting that he knew what was best for his daughter and she felt nothing for him this time. Henry wasn't coming, it would be over soon.

No, they had not suspected her, and she cared not for the shock that would follow when they found her, *a little red will brighten up the place* she thought. It saddened her deeply to know that this would be the last room her eyes would see, it broke her heart that she had not been able to see either of her beautiful girls, or Henry. Where was Henry? He promised that one day he would come back, was he to come back to her now? The time for hoping had shifted and now she relented to doubt and despair, knowing it was the only place that would have her now. She felt the pointed tips under her thumbs, *now is the time* she thought. How many would it take? Would she have the strength to finish what she started?

Then it's in. She is wearing the same linen white dress she wore when they took her, now it is blotching with deep red. After the pain of the penetration subsides, it is replaced with warmth and a calm buzzing. As she watches her life seep away from her she feels herself letting go, wave after wave of relaxation absorbing her. She must do one more, just to make sure, the repercussions could be much worse if she fails to complete the job. She tenderly removes the paintbrush from her abdomen. It has impaled through to the middle of her back, thick blood now oozes from the entry wound.

She begins to feel faint and remembers the last time she saw this much of her own blood. She had been giving birth to her first-born in the kitchen that Henry had painted. He said that doing something with his hands would keep his mind busy and away from anger. It had done, but I knew how he was pacing the wooden corridor, the sound of the slats creaking with every step. Doctor Hammond's wife had recently given birth herself and he was confident in delivering my baby too. He was vowed to secrecy of the birth and he kept his word. Henry had paid him a small sum as a gesture of good will and the Doctor had taken it. Now she impaled herself a second time, but her weak hands could not deliver the same depth of penetration. She had lost velocity as she lacked the strength to push hard, and she winced as it tore her skin slowly. She was comforted by the knowledge that soon it would be over, soon there would be no colour or pain and the Middleton lineage would be free from a sullied name.

***

Doctor Hammond examined Nicole while Jason and Rita searched for Rebecca. Henry knelt beside his daughter, stroking her hair. "I'm here now Nicole, everything is going to be ok." He knew the words that left him were lies.

As far as his daughter's future was concerned now, it lay in the hands of the Doctor. Henry prayed that he could keep Nicole from her Mother's fate, but it was unlikely the good Doctor would accept a bribe. He had seen with his own eyes what she had done to poor Rebecca and he blamed himself. He had turned his beautiful neglected daughter into a monster. What would drive someone to such madness? He thought that maybe she had been jealous of Rebecca. From what he had seen of Rebecca, she was certainly a liar and a thief, but perhaps she had other qualities that Nicole craved. But enough to murder her for? It didn't matter to him. Right now he concentrated on securing a future with his daughter, right now he tried to think of how he was going to tell her. They were startled by the sound of the van engine starting. The van did not pull away but stood still while the engine chugged through the cold air. Jason and Rita heard and came around in a U turn to see what was happening. Jason ran to the passenger's side and wrenched open the rusty door.

Rebecca's hands were grasping the steering wheel, she flailed and reached for the handbrake but Mickey had her in a choke hold. He unclipped her seatbelt and forcefully pulled her over the front seat with one arm wrapped around her throat. How long had he been there, and how did he know where they were? She kicked out in the struggle, her feet denting the dashboard and thumping the windscreen. Suddenly the radio blasted on, it was the Nottingham local news jingle, Henry recognised it hadn't changed in over twenty years. It was the first non-violent communication the four of them had heard all week. "The Baroness of Middleton was found dead in her room early this morning. Nurses and officials say it was not suspicious." The voice echoed from the radio. Doctor Hammond looked at Henry. "I'm so sorry Henry, I wanted to wait until all of this was over, I'm so sorry." Henry's eyes just blinked but there was no life behind them.

He supposed it had been inevitable. Henry had failed

again. Was their incomparable love doomed from the start? He thought so. When two people love each other so much, a sacrifice would have to made at some point. Jason placed a hand on his shoulder, "I'm sorry Henry, if there's anything we can do..." Rita walks from behind the van, dusting off her worked hands. "That lassie's a handful Jason." She points to the back of the van. She obviously hadn't heard the radio announcement amongst the scramble. Rebecca is now bound and gagged to a chair in the back of the van, she is twitching furiously after her foiled escape. Rita dusts off her hands on her long woollen skirt, then stops as the Doctor explains that Eleanor is dead. She crumples to the floor, her oversized cardigan and skirt making her look tiny amongst a mass of clothes. "Oh Henry," she cries, "poor, poor lassie." She already has a handkerchief up her sleeve and pulls it out immediately to blow her nose.

He looks to his daughter. In the beginning he had come to give her a Mother, now he had to take her away, again. His beautiful daughter deserved more than he could give her, how was he supposed to tell her she had lost the Mother she had never even met? How should he describe her beauty, her artistic nature and the intensity of her love? She would never really know. Anyone who had ever met Eleanor would have difficulty forgetting her. He had not stopped thinking about her since the day they first met.

His thoughts were interrupted by gasping from all around him. "Dad?"

"Nicole, what have you done darling?" She tries to lift her head but it's pounding hard. "Did you finish the project Dad, are you back now?" She was delirious. Henry had been away on many 'projects' in the past but Nicole knew he was gone for good last time. She had chosen to remember a happier time, a time when her father had not abandoned her out of self-pity and selfishness. She always was the optimist, he thought. "I'm so sorry darling, you're all I have left now," he wept.

Doctor Hammond takes her pulse again, she begins to cough and he knows it doesn't sound good. "Henry, we need to get Nicole to the hospital right away." He is acting with urgency, already lifting Nicole to her feet, but she can't stand yet. "Who's Henry..." she slurs as they adjust to her weight. "Which hospital?" Henry asks, taking the weight of Nicole over his shoulder. He can't think about explaining everything until she is safe. "It's just to get her checked over Henry, we're going to the Trinity for now." he reassures Henry. He looks over his shoulder to Rita. "Do you know the way to Rampton secure unit?" "I've been there many times me lad!" she shouts back in between sniffles. "Take her there. Tell them I sent you." Jason and Mickey walk around the back of the van and close a door each, she penetrates their eyes the whole time. They continue around to the front, Rita is driving. "How many days was I out for?" Mickey asks, slightly dazed by the recent events. "I'll explain everything on the way." Jason smiles.

As they make their way past the derelict warehouse, they

notice the smoke has deteriorated into small puffs now, the fire must be smouldering now. Henry prays that no do-gooder Joe Public has called the authorities as they manoeuvre Nicole into Doctor Hammond's Clio. Henry sits in the back with her, he can't think where to begin. "What were you trying to achieve here Nicole? You could end up in prison for this." He knew he had been away from his daughter too long and that he didn't have the right to preach, but he wanted to know what was going on. "Where are we?" she said, as if it was nothing to do with her. "You brought Rebecca here, you were trying to change her. In your own little twisted way, I think you were actually trying to help her," he gestured, as if would help her understand. "I remember Jason asking me...that was months ago, I told him no, I told him no! Why don't I remember anything? Why is everyone in the woods, I don't understand..." She sobbed heavily as the shock of what Henry told her, and everything that had happened, began to take its toll on her body. Her brain felt as though it had swelled to the size of melon, it was a groggy feeling, occasionally pierced with a sharpness striking straight through the centre.

"Nicole, do you remember me?"

"Yes, you're my Doctor." she answered.

"Do you remember coming to see me about a month ago?" James was looking at her through the rear view mirror, she had no idea where he was driving them. "I know I came to see you but I couldn't tell you when it was." She shakes her head, worrying there is something that no-one is telling her. "The day you came to see me, I told you the same thing I had told you twice previously." He was maintaining eye contact with her and she hoped the car in front didn't slam its brakes on. "She's blocking the information, that's why you keep forgetting," he tells her. "Who is blocking what information?" She is already confused. "Bernadette." the Doctor says avidly. Bernadette, Bernadette, she thinks back to the amount of times she has heard that name, or thought she has heard that name. That night she and Jason went drinking together, it sounded like that's what he called her. Perhaps he had mistaken her for someone else?

Doctor Hammond, James, could see her struggling to understand what it meant. "You are Bernadette, Nicki. She is a separate entity living inside your body. You created her to guild when Nell told you that you were adopted." She looks to Henry. "You're not my father? Nell's not my mum?" This was far more difficult than Henry had ever imagined it would be. He decided to skip the delicate delivery and just say it.

"Your Mother gave you to me when you were a baby. I was already living with Nell and we were to be married soon, so we raised you together. I was living under a false name at the time to keep me out of the limelight and you both took on that name, Singer." He waited patiently for her to something, he wasn't even sure if she could process it all but after everything that had happened he had to try, he would not risk leaving it until it was too late. After all, it was because of Henry's waiting that she would never meet her Mother. After a minute, she spoke. "If Nell isn't my Mother, then who is?"

Finally, she had reason. The news she had heard from both the Doctor and her Father would send any normal person into a pit of despair, a crazed frenzy of loneliness, but for her it all made sense. For years she had felt alone, like she didn't belong to anything, it was the reason she clung so dearly to the historical interests she shared with her Father. When she looked at Nell she never saw a part of herself, not even in their closest times. Now, finally she could answer the questions she had buried deep within herself. Perhaps knowing who her Mother was would help her complete the puzzle, perhaps for the first time in eighteen years she would feel whole again.

"We're nearly there," Doctor Hammond spoke over his shoulder. "Henry, are you ok mate, Henry stay with us." He took a sharp left into Derby Road and Henry fell onto Nicole, clutching his chest. "Nicole talk to him, you're going to be alright Henry just hang on in there." The Doctor was driving furiously through the traffic. He mounted his blue cherry on the roof of his Saab and put his foot down again. He was looking up at her, smiling through the pain. Henry's heart was giving out on him again and he didn't know if he could last the journey. "Dad, don't go," she wept, "I feel like I've only just found you." She strokes his hair tenderly; she doesn't feel any resentment, only love. His whole body begins to jump, with each fit his limbs become stiff and hardened. She wants to be brave for him but she cries at the thought of losing the love of her life.

So many years she had waited for his return, so many times she has thought of him when admiring her city. Who will understand when he is gone, will she be able to turn to her Mother in his absence? She wondered why her Mother hadn't tried to reach her, hadn't tried to reach Henry. Perhaps she was unwanted then and unwanted now. Nicole had no idea that Eleanor meant for Henry to return with their daughter. She had thought that on seeing their baby, he would return to her after their separated nine months. He squeezed her hand tightly and saw Eleanor. She was certainly as beautiful, if not more so, and he longed to be with her. "No Dad, you can't leave," she pleaded, but Henry was already resting in his wife's arms.

Doctor Hammond brought the car to a halt right outside the Trinity. He had called ahead to ensure a doctor was on standby when they arrived. They were understaffed and underpaid but Hammond's family commanded respect, being the main proprietors of the Trinity for over fifty years. Many of the senior staff told James how they had had the pleasure of working with his Father. Now that his Father was gone, James had made a personal pledge to follow strongly in his footsteps. His Father was the only reason he helped the Middletons now. It was what his Father had done for Eleanor and her first-born, now he would do the same for Henry and his daughter. Whenever he was in doubt, he just asked what his Father would have done. When he had originally tried to institutionalize Nicole, it had only ever been about her own safety. He knew if he put her somewhere that his jurisdiction outweighed theirs, she would be safe. He knew he had failed by her then, and now her Father was dying.

They followed him in as they hurriedly wheeled the stretcher through the hospital entrance. Henry breathed deeply into the face mask. Every so often he would come around, remove his face mask and reach for Nicole. She would smile and find his hand, squeezing tight. They came to a stop at a set of double swing doors with slim rectangular windows in them. It was the operating theatre. Nicole knew that once her Father went in, there was every chance she may never see him again. He still hadn't told her who she was.

The intercom buzzed. "Henry Middleton for open heart with Nick," the nurse said into the speaker. The door buzzed open and she began to walk in backwards, pulling Henry on the stretcher. "Please," begged Nicole, "I've only just found him!" she cried. She was still holding his hand, he wouldn't let go. James put a hand on her shoulder. "They need to act now Nicki, otherwise there is no hope." With that, Henry released his grip and his hand fell heavily onto the bed. She watched them lift his body from the stretcher and up onto the operating theatre. The surgeon was waiting for the anaesthetist to finish before he could start opening Henry's chest with a saw which he held in his right hand. Normally this would not be acceptable behaviour in front of a patient, but Henry was barely conscious and the surgeon had to act fast. A nurse in blue scrubs pulled the curtain around Henry as James' phone began ringing, he paced down the squeaky marble corridor to take the call.

He saw Nicole being ushered away from the gruesome events about to start in the operating theatre and into the waiting room. It was the secure unit at Rampton, they had called to verify Rebecca's admission to the premises. He told them he would check on her himself once he had finished with business here. He made his way to the waiting room and sat tentatively next to Nicole. "It will be ok Nicki, the surgeons here are excellent," he smiled. James had only been on the phone for five minutes but Nicole had lost all concept of time. She felt guilty that her Father lay on an operating table fighting for his life and all she could think about was her Mother. Who was she, why had she given her away and why hadn't she tried to find her? If her Father couldn't tell her who she was, then who could?

It had taken them fifteen minutes to saw through Henry's sternum, now Henry lay upon the operating theatre, his vital organs on show to the surgeons.

He was anesthetized but Henry could still hear everything. He even heard the distant sound of the monitor droning as he flat-lined. He couldn't feel it but after that Nick was massaging his heart, willing it to start beating again; no surgeon wants to lose a patient on his table, but it was too late.

In his mind he saw her. She waited for him there, her porcelain face searching for him at the window and lighting up when she sees him racing down the drive.

Her face pales as she sees the way the Doctor is approaching her. He has removed the bandanna that he had worn in surgery, now he holds it delicately between his hands, his blood-stained scrubs remaining in the operating wash room. It looks to her as though Nick has said what he is about to say a million times over already. "I'm so sorry Nicole, we couldn't save him. We did everything we could but his heart just gave up. There are some personal effects he wanted you to have, when you're ready you can collect them from the reception on floor five." James followed him out. He didn't wait for her to ask any questions, but just directed a nurse towards her, and together they walked to a separate room, away from people and the general noise of the hospital. She looked over her shoulder as the door closed behind them, and she heard Nick say, "I'm sorry for your loss James, I know he was a patient of yours."

***

They had cleaned and dressed Rebecca's wound, all the while with her screaming that her name was Susie, and eventually they had taken the easy route and sedated her, much quieter for everyone; even though they were in a separate building of the hospital now, soon she would be moved to her room and they didn't want to risk her riling the other patients. She awoke in her room, it had been the only one available on such short notice, it was situated at the quieter end of the wing. The ceiling was white and she became bored instantly, trying to get up off of the bed to have a look around. Rebecca accepted that she needed to be here, after all they may be able to help her gain control of Susie. She had ruined her life. She was in it so much that a stranger would think that Rebecca was the weak personality! This was her body damn it and she wanted it to stay that way, she was fed up of sharing. Mac had not even tried to find her. She had no idea how long she was kept in that warehouse, he wouldn't have noticed her missing until he wanted his glass refilling.

When she had seen where they were on arrival, she thought about the last time she was here. She had followed Mac to try and find out where the money was coming from. The money never did make it straight in to her account, she knew that Mac had somehow convinced whoever it was to change their mind. She wondered if she would meet them now, now that she was in. With one big push she hurls herself up off the bed, the valium is making it hard to move, her muscles feel like jelly. The musty lino is the first thing she notices. A tiny hole in the wall they call a window, would she be getting her hour a day outside for exercise? She hoped so if that was all the daylight she was going to see in here.

There were some colourful paintings on the wall, they

looked a little amateur but she liked them. She walks five paces from the window to the bed, trying not to move the bandages around her legs, and smells the linen. It is freshly washed, at least she had a clean bed. She edges herself onto it once more, deciding that a rest will probably do her good and on waking next time she won't feel so groggy. Laying her head on the pillow she hears a crunching sound. She feels under her pillow, hoping it isn't a cockroach. After searching through the pillow case, she withdraws a photograph. She stares in disbelief at the person in the photo. She can remember the day it was taken at school, it was the day of the balloon race, she was eight years old. She turned over the picture. On the other side read the initials; E.J.M.

***

It plagued her as they walked solemnly down to floor five. According to Nick, Doctor Hammond's Father had treated Henry in the past. "So your father knew my father?" She eventually said, her voice booming out next to her thoughts. "Yes, he knew your Mother too." Finally, she thought, someone who could tell her who her Mother was. They were at the reception now. "Nicole Singer to collect her father's possessions?" James said, leaning over the counter. Hearing the name 'Singer' sent her head into a whirlwind. From now on Nicole would change her name to that of Middleton. Maybe then her Mother would be able to track her down.

The receptionist had a kind face, she smiled gently as she

passed Henry's belongings over the counter in a clear plastic bag. She could already see a gold Rolex and a wallet containing at least a hundred pounds, it was becoming clear that her father had been a wealthy man. She wondered what else he had been keeping from her. Reaching inside the bag, her hand found a photograph. She pulled it out hoping it would be a photo of her father. After he left, Nell had removed any trace of him ever being there, even the one she hid under her pillow at night. 'Eleanor Jane Middleton' it read along the back. She flipped it over in her hand. "That is your Mother," James whispers as they exit the hospital.

Chapter Eighteen: End Game

"She's beautiful." Nicole was still pawing over the photograph of Eleanor, her coffee going cold. They had made it across the street to a quaint little cafe. She was waiting for James to tell her about Eleanor but he just kept asking her if she was ok. All she wanted to do was scream at him that she was fine and just get him to tell her what was going on.

Now that they were in a quiet place where she couldn't run he would tell her. It was a risk he didn't want to take in public, if Bernadette were to show up in a crowded area he would not be able to protect Nicole. "Nicki, my father knew of both your parents." He thought about how his father had told him the story of delivering for James' Mother and Eleanor in the same day. It was not for him to divulge the family secrets, he would only tell her what she needed to know. She was already nodding, anxious to hear more. "Your Mother suffered from severe depression and when it was clear that Henry couldn't help her he had her admitted to Rampton. Your father never liked to speak of it but in his statement he spoke of not knowing who he would wake up with, woman or beast. Do not misunderstand Nicole, your father loved Eleanor deeply but he didn't know how to help her." James was sitting with his elbows resting on the table, his hands offering up the sky as he explained.

"Are you saying that my condition could have been inherited?"

"I never treated your Mother, and my Father died before I began treating you, but yes, it looks as though that could be the case." She nods frantically now, her eyes searching for the next question. "Can I go to see her?" She asks hopefully. "It seems your Mother's condition worsened of late..." He pauses, not quite knowing how to break it to her, he knows he must be careful, telling Nicole is not like telling anyone else. "Just tell me James, I'm so fed up with being lied to, all anyone that I have ever loved has done lately is lied to me. Please just tell me the truth!" "Ok, I'm sorry, calm down, deep breaths." He shushes her, she is already becoming tearful. "They found Eleanor in the early hours this morning. She had stabbed herself twice using one of her paintbrushes." Silence. That was it. Her mind was clear. It had been overloaded with emotion, confusion and information, and now it just shut down.

"I would've killed her you know," she spat across the table. James had been expecting her. "Thank goodness you didn't, otherwise I'd be having a much harder job of keeping Nicole out of prison right now." "Where is the bitch anyway?"

"Rebecca is at Rampton, luckily there is no lasting damage." He wants to ask her what the hell she thought she was doing, torturing Rebecca half to death, nearly landing Nicole with a prison sentence. He wanted to tell her that she should have left her with him, he could have treated her properly. "Hopefully she'll die in there like Eleanor, then Nicki won't need to see any of them again. She can rely on me." Her eyes flashed blank for a second and then she was gone.

"Do they know why she did it?" Nicki asked. "No," he answers, shaking his head, "your Mother would never speak to anyone, let alone confide in them. I have yet to speak to the therapist but if there is a reason we'll find it." He smiles. "Don't worry Nicole, we're not going to let your condition get to that point, your mother was at the point where she wouldn't have recognised herself in a mirror. We still have time for you." His hands are now resting on her shoulders and she can feel herself trying not to cry.

The cemetery work men stood back from the pit. It had taken them the course of a week to dig, the rain thwarting their every attempt. It was a big job too, double burial they had been told, a full six by twelve. They'd had no choice but to dig through the night, twenty-four hours surrounded by mud and water. It hadn't rained last night, but now pellets of water hit the ground with force and cascading waterfalls fed into the depths. Soon it would be full, soon her parents would be filling the earthy void.

Jason had told Rita everything. Much of it had been more difficult than when he had come out to her, but he knew it was for the best. They had dropped Rebecca at Rampton and headed back toward the city. It had been plenty of time for Jason to explain the backward thinking behind their kidnapping of Rebecca. Rita had known how much Jason had loved Stan; she had ruined that for them, and although she was a proud Catholic woman, there was understanding in her eyes as he explained.

She had been living with them for a week.

Doctor Hammond had been sure to explain the complexities of the situation, the magnitude of taking in a schizophrenic patient, and explain that Nicole would be far more susceptible to an episode at this challenging time. Rita had agreed that it wasn't a problem and had taken a month's leave from her job as a care assistant to watch over her. Rita had asked Jason out of curiosity when it had all began. Jason said, "The day it felt like it was never going to stop raining, the day that Henry left." Rita remembered, she recalled how Nicki had asked for Jason that day, an unusual thing for Nicole to do, but she had put it down to the shock of losing her father.

She thinks to the present, today is the day of the funeral. She hopes today they can lay Bernadette to rest.

The journey in the car had been quiet. Nobody knew quite what to say. Rita reined in her own grief and remained strong for Nicole. She had been a shell of herself since Henry died, but there was a calmness about her that Rita hadn't seen before. Even though recent events had shocked her, she thought Nicole could at least put her doubts to rest now. Rita had prayed every night that they would not see the return of Bernadette.

There were only a handful of people at the service, James Hammond being one of them, and despite the rain it had been held outside. Rita explained to Nicole that the Middleton family had abandoned her parents after Eleanor became sick. She was choosing the right moment to explain the cause of Eleanor's illness, Nicole had been sick at the sight of the two coffins laid side by side. It was a small wave of black that said Goodbye to Henry and Eleanor Middleton, and said that even though they were at peace now, their secrets lived on.

Epilogue

The distant sound of the phone ringing slowly brought her attention back to the present. She had been thinking about starting work again soon and moving back into her house on Citadel Street. It had been three weeks since the funeral. Rita's footsteps climbed the stairs. Jason had been there for her through it all, feeling that it was his fault for coercing her into the whole mess. He said if it hadn't been for his want for revenge, Nicki would never have been involved. It was difficult for her to know the truth. Bernadette had obviously set a vendetta of her own, from what Doctor Hammond had told her, it seemed unlikely that she would have needed much persuasion. She had forgiven Jason everything; after all, who else would have stuck by a friend with split personality disorder? He was all she had. Rita opened the door to Jason's room where she had been sleeping, "You're to go to the lawyer's office for the reading of the Will."

"When?"

"Tomorrow."

Typical she thought. Just as she had begun trying to piece her life back together, it was ready to fall apart again. Tonight she would barely sleep at all.

***

Tomorrow she was being taken down town, they wouldn't tell her why on account of they didn't want her getting 'excited'. Rebecca had learnt that in here, that meant out of control, and out of control meant sedation. In the three weeks she had been here, she had not seen Susie once. Susie was a coward. Rebecca felt nothing but anger and disgust whenever she thought of her. Susie had only ever appeared when there was something to steal or a person she could bend to her will. She had made Rebecca's life a living hell. Unfortunately she dominated Rebecca; Susie was a stronger character, and the only reason she was absent now was because there was nothing here for her to have. That is unless she planned on stealing the other psych patients' chocolate mousse. She wondered if it was her hearing that they were be taking her to tomorrow. Whatever it is, she thought, I hope Susie stays here.

***

Standing in front of the full length mirror in Rita's room, she held up her picture of Eleanor. Nicole had put on her prettiest dress in memory of the Mother she had never met. "You're a bonnie lass Nicki, your Mother would be proud. You look just like her, don't ya think?" Rita was standing behind her. She hoped that Nicole would not lose trust in her after the Will had been read. Rita had decided it was not her place to disclose the family secrets, and she knew Jesus would find a way into her heart. Nicole smiled back at her through the mirror, "I do don't I? Eleanor was beautiful." "And so are you babe, don't you worry about that lassie." Rita said, placing a kiss on Nicki's forehead. Now they were ready to leave.

***

They were Rampton's answer to armed guards; two stocky guys loaded with hypodermic tranqs escorted Rebecca downtown. Her first outing with them had been to the Trinity for surgery on her legs, the nurses at Rampton had taken care of the cuts on her head after sedating her on arrival. She sat squished in the middle of the broad men, in the back of a Meriva people carrier. As they made a left turn into Fletcher Gate, she realised it wasn't the County Courts they were visiting. The car came to a gentle stop, so as not to 'excite' anyone, outside the Palmer Offices. "This is your stop Miss," said Archer from the front seat, he was trying to be comical and it did cheer her a little. With her guards on either side, she made her way up the cobbled footpath to the old Edwardian building.

The trip down to Fletcher Gate had taken less time than usual, and they arrived early for their appointment. The lawyer had informed them that James would be there. Rita waited in reception as the assistant showed Nicole through to Peter's office. James was already inside chatting to Peter, they both stopped and looked up at her as she stepped into the cosy room. It was not modern and stuffy as she had imagined, but filled with artefacts from all over the world. She could see why her father had chosen Peter. "Hi Nicole, I'm Peter Douglas, I'll be reading your parents' will today." He smiled and gave Nicole a firm hand shake. Peter was tall and broad, and despite being in his early fifties, Nicole guessed, the jet black hair was all his own. She noticed the skin on his hands was supple and soft, not unlike his mannerisms. "Hello again Nicki," James greeted her. She smiled warmly, and they chatted for a while about menial subjects while they waited for the meeting to begin. She took the seat next to James, somehow feeling safer when he was around. After several minutes of Nicole looking around the room, Peter read her confused expression and told her, "We're just waiting for one more person Miss Middleton."

She nodded and smiled, even though she had no idea who he was referring to. Her mind searched frantically for the possible third person, but came up empty. Then, a knock at the door. Peter rose to his feet swiftly and made his way to the oak wood door. Standing on the other side was what looked like a security guard, a statuesque man dressed in black, wearing something around his waist that looked similar to a tool belt. They exchanged a few words at the door then Peter stepped aside to admit the guard... followed by Rebecca. Silence struck the room as Nicole and Rebecca locked eyes, each as shocked as the other to be in the same room again. James is observing both of them carefully. Peter takes a deep breath. "So does everyone know each other?" Peter's voice cracked the silence. James watches them both as they nod in Peter's direction, never taking their eyes from one another. "Ok, now that everyone is here we can begin," Peter smiled.

After they had each completed the formalities required

before listening to Eleanor Jane Middleton's and Henry Herbert Middleton's last Will and Testament, Peter explained he would read a statement from Eleanor. Rebecca was thinking about how the initials on her wall at Rampton had matched the ones on the cheques she had found, addressed to Mac when she was only sixteen. If the money from those cheques had been meant for her... she hadn't seen a penny.

Peter read:

To my beautiful daughters, it is only now that I may address you as such. It warms my blood just to say it aloud, my baby girls. I have longed to see you for such a time, but I couldn't wait any more. My heart aches with each lonely memory, empty time frames that should have been filled with the laughter of children. I could bare it no longer and now you must know that I have departed from your world.

Please love each other in our absence as we should have loved you. You are all that is left of Henry and I, I wish to no longer hide behind the mistakes of the past. Wear your Middleton inheritance with pride as I once did. I dearly hope it will serve you both better than the fate it carved for my beloved Henry and I.

To my first born.

Rebecca, I only know your name because your father visited me with your photograph, I keep it in my pillow case so that you can visit me in my dreams. Your father assured me you were receiving my maintenance, I hope it has seen you well. I can only hope that you understand it was a different time when you were born. Although my meeting with your father was purely a mistake, you were always a gift and one that I long to cherish. It is my greatest wish that you care for your sister, blood is all you both have now. To you, my daughter Rebecca, I give the sum of five hundred thousand pounds to do with what you please. I know that no amount of money can ever make up for the absence of a Mother but I hope it will pave the way to a happier future for you and your family.

To my second born,

My dear Nicole, you were never meant to leave me. It was my naivety that led the way to a life without my daughter. Your father was meant to bring you back and live with me until we were old and grey, but when he looked upon your face it merely reminded him of my betrayal. He never brought you back to me and I miss you sorely. To you, Nicole, I leave the Wollaton Hall Estate. Perhaps you could feel close to me here and love it as dearly as I have. Think of me as you gaze upon the deer my love.

To James Hammond, family Doctor and friend:

Dear James, you have always done right by our family,

even when it has meant possibly damaging your own good name. When our own kind abandoned us you were there through it all. It is my sincere wish that you continue to watch over our family and protect them. In honour of you and your family's persistent loyalty and courage, please accept a sum in the amount of ten thousand pounds.

The room is stilled and quiet. Peter pauses for a sip of water, looking at each one of their faces as he does so. They seem stunned by the voices of the dead. Peter was used to many things, celebrations, happiness, but he was not used to silence at the reading of a will. He picked up the next piece of paper from his desk. "From Henry," he said, and continued to read aloud:

To my dear Nicole, I leave you the Wollaton Hall Estate and the title 'Baroness of Middleton', a title long preceded by your Mother. I still regret the day I chose to walk away from you and I deeply regret leaving you as a child. Please do not place blame with your Mother, after the first baby she was not herself. We couldn't fight our way back to the way it was before, no matter how hard we tried.

I hope you will love living at Wollaton, I know you visited many times as a child, it nearly killed me not being able to tell you that it would be yours some day. If only I could be there to see you arrive.

I have been at war with myself since that fatal day Eleanor left you with me, but now, finally I can be with her and at peace. I hope that you will find peace now Nicole, until we meet again, your father Henry.

The room is silent again. For the first time they looked upon each other now and saw their faces reflected. Rebecca's hair was beginning to grow back now, and soon it would resemble the beechy waves Nicole had seen in Eleanor's photograph.

After everything they had been through, with everything they still had left to conquer, they looked at each other and finally saw someone to share their madness.

www.ingramcontent.com/pod-product-compliance
Lightning Source LLC
Chambersburg PA
CBHW050036180626
46810CB00002B/749